UNVEILED

The First Unthank School Anthology

UNTHANK

First Published in 2019
by Unthank Books

All Rights Reserved. A CIP record for this book is available from the British Library.

Any resemblance to persons fictional or real who are living, dead or undead is purely coincidental

ISBN 978-1-910061-55-8

Edited by Ashley Stokes and Stephen Carver

Jacket Design by Robot Mascot
www.robotmascot.co.uk

Typesetting and layout by Michelle Collin

Lost Lessons of Imaginary Men © Nicola Perry 2019
Walls © Sabine Meier 2019
Inference © Susan Allott 2019
In Control © Jose Varghese 2019
Writer © Jax Burgoyne 2019
The Red King © Nicholas Brodie 2019
No Second Chances © Carey Denton 2019
Ideas I am sending on Holiday © Claudie Whittaker 2019
Roads © John Down 2019
To Sudden Silence Won © Jacqueline Gittins 2019
The Lantern Man © Victoria Hattersley 2019
Zoldana © Zoe Fairlough 2019
The Shadow of Moths © Lorraine Rogerson 2019
Killing Coldplay © Marc Owen Jones 2019
Shizuko © Lloyd Mills 2019

www.unthankbooks.com

CONTENTS

Introduction:
The book that you hold in your hands .... Ashley Stokes

Lost Lessons of Imaginary Men .... Nicola Perry **3**

Walls .... Sabine Meier **17**

Inference .... Susan Allott **31**

In Control .... Jose Varghese **43**

Writer .... Jax Burgoyne **57**

The Red King .... Nicholas Brodie **71**

No Second Chances .... Carey Denton **85**

Ideas I am sending on Holiday .... Claudie Whittaker **93**

Roads .... John Down **103**

To Sudden Silence Won .... Jacqueline Gittins **115**

The Lantern Man .... Victoria Hattersley **125**

Zoldana .... Zoe Fairlough **137**

The Shadow of Moths .... Lorraine Rogerson **149**

Killing Coldplay .... Marc Owen Jones **163**

Shizuko .... Lloyd Mills **173**

INTRODUCTION

The book that you hold in your hands

All revolutions start with five people meeting in an upstairs room. It will be raining outside and early in the week as well as the year. Christmas decorations will have not long been put back in their boxes. One of the lights won't be working. One of the windows will rattle. Some of the assembled are caught up in a grand dream already, and some only here to explore the possibilities. Some are old hands, some novices. Everyone has something that they want to contribute. Everyone has something to say and something to share.

This was the atmosphere that surrounded the first ever Unthank School of Writing workshop, which took place in January 2011 at the York Tavern in Norwich. And like all revolutions, this one has produced a book.

The book that you hold in your hands contains stories that brim with the storytelling verve, imagination and talent of writers we have supported during the first seven years of the Unthank School. All are the product of hard work and commitment and all will tell you something about what we are about and what we cultivate.

A brief history of the Unthank School

The Unthank School was founded both as an accompaniment to Unthank Books, and as a direct response to the cutting of community creative writing after the 2008 crash.

Several of us had been working as associate lecturers in creative writing for many years. As austerity swept its scythe through the system, the university departments that had provided us with employment disbanded around us (without any warning in some cases). Creative writing in the community was becoming a thing of the past. Believing that writing is for everyone, we didn't want to let this happen.

We started by offering an Introduction to Writing Fiction to provide new writers with a basic grounding in terms, techniques and practice, and an Advanced Fiction Workshop for writers with work in progress, both of which have been taught by Sarah Bower and Ashley Stokes. We did initially offer screenwriting and poetry courses, and even ran one term of poetry, but it soon became obvious that fiction was our thing, no doubt because we were connected to a fiction publisher. As such, we added a twenty-five week Writing the Novel course. However, we didn't abandon other forms of writing altogether. Later we were joined by Lilie Ferrari, who ran an introduction and workshops in writing for TV drama, soaps and serials. In 2015, Stephen Carver became part of the team and took us online. Stephen now teaches a much praised How to Write a Novel course. The online version of the evening, face-to-face workshop in Norwich, the Online Fiction Workshop, taught by Stephen and Ashley, found an international as well as a British constituency. In 2018 we were joined by the extremely experienced writer and tutor, Tom Vowler, who has added online courses specifically for short story writers to the school. Our latest recruit is Georgina Parfitt, who teaches the Norwich introductory class. It's frequently fed back to us that no one teaches creative writing like Unthank.

The long game of becoming a better writer
Although we had all benefited from teaching creative writing for universities and art schools – and many of us still do – we were able, outside of the institutional setting, to ditch elements of university teaching that we felt served little purpose or inhibited writers, namely grading, tickbox assessments, self-reflective appraisals, and too much emphasis on close-reading and line-editing. Close-reading and editing are important, obviously, but with new writers or writers working on a first draft, excessive comma patrol and quibbling about usage can suck the life out of a promising story that's not yet found its flow. There's no point chopping off fingers that are still groping towards the light. Instead, in workshops at least, we focus on storytelling and listening to the writer discuss what he or she intends for the story and helping to shape an unfolding narrative.

It is interesting, in this light, that most Unthank School tutors have had some, or lots, of experience working for The Literary Consultancy, under the feathers of the late, irreplaceable Rebecca Swift and now Aki Schilz. Here, we have worked with full-length manuscripts and with every type of writer and novel, from the most brutally boilerplate thrillers to 900-page experimental tracts written backwards in the lost language of cranes. The scope of this editorial work has allowed us to develop a practical and flexible approach to teaching writing, one that isn't about the syllabus or the canon or the network, but what pitfalls wait the unwary writer who pushes ahead without input or feedback.

Unthank's cure is very much a talking cure and uses the example of the writer's own work to teach from. We pride ourselves on being eclectic and responsive. We prompt and pre-empt. We try to make things work for the writers, so their stories realise themselves on their own terms.

Another advantage we found we have is that we spend far more time with our students, especially online, and more time in terms of weekly contact hours. It becomes far, far easier to build a rapport with our students. Conversations often range widely, attacking a subject by digression, going off-piste only to come back to the point with a new and surprising possibility. These workshops are terrifically entertaining and can be the most fun anyone has when he or she is talking about their writing. The workshops are rolling and run three times a year. This means that we do see novels grow from idea to finished draft. With students who stay for the long haul, we get to see these novels through the drafting process. At the moment, we are seeing quite a few students start a second book. Some of our students, like Catharine Barter and Annie Beaumont have had books published with mainstream publishers or via the self-publishing route.

We have become proud of the work that the school produces, impressed by the wit, doggedness and inventiveness of our students. It is this that inspired us to put out a call for submissions for Unveiled. We received writing from over fifty former and current students. The fifteen stories here are the ones we felt are the most realised, the stories with the most authoritative voices, that demanded that we include them.

Beautiful sparks

For many of the writers here, this is their first brush with printer's ink. For some it is the first time they have submitted a story to a publisher. For others, it's the first time they have been accepted by a publisher. Most of the stories here are novel extracts, which means that they need a little contextualising if they're not first chapters, so a little precis precedes where necessary. The stories range from Berlin to Australia to the British street and beyond. Here, there are introverts and psychopaths, frustrated housewives and perplexed old men. There are time-slips and childhood trauma, historical fictions, speculative fictions and slices of life, an abundance of stories. No creative writing school can guarantee success for its students and certainly not in all the forms that publishing success can take. For some, though, this may be the first in a long line of publications. What we have in Unveiled is a profusion of beautiful sparks, glinting fragments, wonderful suggestions. Each of these tasters and samples hints at something greater to follow.

The Editors

LOST LESSONS OF IMAGINARY MEN

NICOLA PERRY

Imagine a place where an old man can tell fairy tales to teenage boys, and they listen; a street artist can stalk a woman, pass through walls and become the hunted one, and a Moth can defy every expectation to become a man. These are the stories septuagenarian Eddie Donoghue – failed New Yorker, failed artist, failed family man, and failing human being – needs you to hear. For the funny thing about failures is they can have a way of surprising you.

PROLOGUE
A Boy's Lessons in Seven Imaginings

Lesson I

My mother is dead inside. There's nothing I can do for her. I am instructed in this from a young age. Ari, my son, there's nothing you can say, do or think that will ever make me feel your love, mama tells me over and over, brushing the fringe from my eyes – her gestures only ever ones of neatening. She does not say this to be cruel. She says this to release me from all duty to be the one to make her happy.

Love, she says, one day as we are riding on a bus from somewhere wet to somewhere dry, is a word people dish out to measure out their pleasure and displeasure. She warns me for the longest time not to love her – because it kills her to know what I feel depends on her.

Lesson II

Men and women can murder one another without lifting a hand. It is my father's mother, Gigi, who teaches me this, the year before papa and I leave the Ukraine for America. I am seven. She is standing in her kitchen peeling potatoes with a sharp paring knife over a bubbling pan of hot water when she instructs me, People can murder without their victims being buried in the ground. How to make sense of a thing like this. That a thing can be both dead and living at the same time. But I nod to show I understand. I do not tell her that I know because my mother – her son's old wife – is dead inside. Because I understand no one wants to be fed uncooked spuds. I think somehow this is love.

Lesson III

From when I am a small boy, I notice how women do not look at me in the same way they look at other children. With others, a lady may widen her eyes and smile or make comical faces. With me, they are stone. When they look down, they stare through me. When I move along the street, they flow away from me. When I am eight years old, I tell my mother that women are afraid of me. Nonsense, she says, women are afraid of two things: grown men and themselves. Mama says it is because every woman is looking for a smile; and until I give them what they want, they will punish me by withholding theirs. Nonsense, Gigi says, raising her voice, if women go still around the boy, then the boy must pay attention to what it is they do not want him to see. To which my mother sighs, Oh, the oracle has spoken. Pulling me close – the whiskers on her upper lip poking in my ear – Gigi insists When a woman doesn't want to be seen, there is always a reason. But she gives my mother credit for one thing – when a woman is afraid of a child, it is because she is afraid for herself. So, I begin to pay attention…

Lesson IV

The first girl I practice on is a large, dimpled girl who serves us our meat at the butchers. Each Friday, mama and I stand with the other women and children on our side of the counter as the butcher hands the bloody meat to the dimpled girl, his assistant. It is her task to wrap the meat. She is younger than the other women who come and go. Her face is rounder and softer. Too round, too soft, I hear the women around us complain. I think they think they are whispering.

Eye level with the girl's hands, I peer through the counter glass, admiring, as her fingers smooth the paper, coaxing the meat, deftly folding the edges until each parcel is a gift. My grandmother would say she is someone who takes pride in her work. But, as the people around us jostle to get closer to the counter, a chorus picks up. What's the hold up? Why so slow today? I jump when the butcher shouts at the girl – What do I pay you for? To daydream?

I look on as the butcher looms over the girl, minding her every move. If I were my grandmother, I'd tell the man off, correct him. No dreamer folds like that. But I am not Gigi. I want to reach through the glass and touch the girl's hands, but all I can do is press my two palms to the glass. Above my head, I hear a single voice rise above the din. Please tell your boy not to dirty the glass. I look up and see it is the dimpled girl speaking over me. Mama grips my shoulders and I drop away.

The following Friday, something happens and I must be elsewhere.

Lesson V

Friday, I don't like Gigi's funeral. I don't like that she is not there. It is very lonely without her, or mama, there. My titka, my father's sister, holds my hand. But I wriggle away. She has no grip. Not like mama's or Gigi's. Almost like there was no one holding my fingers at all. Afterwards, back at Gigi's apartment, all my uncles go stand out in the hallway, and my father orders me to go play. But there is no one to play with. So, I go looking for a woman. This time I study my titka. I find her leaning against the railing, outside on the balcony, looking out over the sad, half spires and rooftops of our city. All the other women are inside busying themselves. Gigi always said titka had idle hands. I think how different titka is from the butcher's assistant, who is far superior. I stand in the doorway, neither in nor out, watching, waiting for her to notice there is someone with her. As long as I can remember, I have been lost to titka in a haze of her cigarette smoke. Today though is different; the only pollution is rising up from the street, but still I cough. Reluctantly, she turns away from the view, placing her idle hands in her pockets, facing me in the doorway. Has she been crying? Her cold gaze cuts through me, as if there were someone coming up behind me she didn't like. I turn, but there is no one there. She begins talking for my benefit, because I am there. But her mouth is strange. If I were to touch her lips, they would be marble. Everyone busy inside? The women cooking? The menfolk talking between feedings? Before turning her back on me, she adds, Anything but idleness, eh?

Lesson VI

We do not go to the butchers for many Fridays. I do not know why. I think it is because mama has lost her appetite. Then one Friday, she sends me there, alone, with a note. I know not to pass this to the butcher because he is a busy man. I wait for the dimpled girl but she is nowhere to be seen. The new assistant is all elbows and efficiency. I wait for the other women ahead of me to be served, knowing to move forward with the crowd. It is only when I reach the counter, and get to peer through the glass, and see the deft folding of the edges of each bloody parcel that I realise this is the dimpled girl. Lifting the note high above my head, I wait for her to take possession. But she is serving someone else, and then another. I wave the note to gain her attention. At first, she hesitates to take the folded article but, as she does so, the butcher brings his knife down hard on the wooden surface beside her, shouting at the girl. What do I pay you for? To pass notes? Frightened, she drops the torn sheet, leaving my mother's words stranded on the counter.

> Months from now, The Painter will say how to not cut
> yourself when everyone is handing you scissors –
> is the hardest love to learn.

But I am not with the painter yet. I am marooned at the butchers. Abruptly, an unseen woman at the back of the crowd pipes up, His mother must have sent him. For godsakes, serve the boy. It is only when the butcher signals that this is ok, that the girl takes up our note. After reading its brief contents, she shakily passes it to the butcher. The whole time, she does not look away from me and I smile back, marvelling. Perhaps this is all it takes to have a woman look at me. Help.

Incredibly, the girl invites me around to her side of the counter and even provides a stool. I could sit by her side all day, staring happily at the immovable dimple in her left cheek.

It surprises me, when some time later, papa walks in. He strides past me and to the counter. He goes straight up to the butcher, who passes him the note. My note. My mother's note. I look on as he unfolds the paper and reads mama's words. I never do learn what is inside. What I do see is that my father cannot look at me. But that's ok, because all I know, as I leave the shop, is how happy I am that the dimple-faced girl held my hand and stroked my fringe. I do not understand that this is because she is more afraid for me than of me, now.

Lesson VII

My father and I do not go to my mother's funeral. A thing like that cannot be honoured, he tells me. Papa makes arrangements for us to go to America instead.

I understand from a young age that my father owns me. That I am on loan to my mother, and that I can be taken back. What I did not know is how he owned my aunt too.

On the drive to the airport, when he tells me he has disowned titka – that the whole family has – what surprises me more is titka's new owner. Not a husband. Nor a blood relation. That, as an unmarried, she is now owned by her unborn child.

I did not know there were adults who could belong to their children. This is a very bad thing, my father warns me.

But what if he is feeding me uncooked spuds?

CHAPTER ONE
The Painter, New York

So few know this about me, but I've been getting off subway stops prematurely for years. It used to be up to fifteen blocks at a pop, thirty at a stretch, but time strains even the strongest of walker's calves. It was my first wife who got me going. After that, well, I guess, it became habit; there being a lot of steam to work off in those days, and not all on the home front. When it morphed from habit into superstition, I couldn't tell you, but I can tell you I like it best how it is now… as my secret to know.

Look up from the shuffle of shoes and I see Upper Manhattan is blue. My god, this light is incredible. Carry on walking the seven blocks up from Broadway and W 110th, I worry ahead of time that I am holding something up somewhere in the Manhattan cosmos, but sometimes a person simply has to come up for air.

Let others honk their car horns whilst you clip past the three-card monte dealers on the corners of the mid 100s, advancing with the crowd; loving that you are in the most vibrant city on earth. Scan the cardboard sign of some homeless guy while he's checking out some woman's legs, before he calls out, 'Love the outfit, shame about the shoes, honey.' See his printed message to the world. Feed me. Subtext. Show me some God-damned Love. Make eye contact with him and shamefully look away.

Breathe in the residue of the vendor's cooking on 47th and frown at some male sales assistant wrestling to keep a female mannequin upright in a department store window. He's so rough with her. What's that about? you wonder.

Anyone ever tell you the story of the lady in the all-male concentration camp?

So, the story goes all the detainees were becoming more beast than men. With nothing to own (not even a future), they'd gone to the dogs fast when one among them began pretending that there was a female present. Pretty soon, they were all pretending. First, they cleaned up their talk, then other civilizing habits returned.

Imagine that. These days, out in the real world, I see more men using woman as their excuse for letting things slide; badmouthing the opposite sex for being less than an institution.

Wait for the crossing to turn to 'man walking' and look up west 165th. The blue is fading.

Stop short after United Palace. We're here. Home. The Towers.

Look up and shore up the immensity of those thirty storeys soaring high above you. The building got itself finished in the nick of time; before the Great Depression hit and The Heights became spoiled goods. I'm on the 23rd floor. Someone in the family has been here since the '80s. Thank God for rent control, and a service elevator that works when the residents' ones don't. The Heights have always been home though, ever since I was a good catholic boy making his way to choir at St Mary's. You can't see my window from way down here, but what a view.

Hear that? Everyone talking Spanish. Quisqueya Heights, they call it now, ever since the Dominicans moved in. Not that I talk much with the neighbors anymore. Some will translate that as me being racist, but there's no class in labelling a thing. We don't talk because we are strangers to one another. Simple as.

No need for the service elevator today. Excuse the graffiti. No matter how many mothers berate their sons, new artists arrive daily. Mind your step on the way out. There's always someone or something looking to trip you up in the hallways. I'm down the far end. Do the smells bother you? Other people's cooking isn't for everyone.

What was I saying before about the sexes? you ask.

Ah yes, what you aren't told as a young man, what few young women understand either, I suppose, is that a man doesn't know how to invite a woman in because, until the world and all its business – in its entirety – drains away, he has no awareness of the immeasurable space inside him. The world has convinced him that all the space is taken.

This is me.

You're hesitating. It's perfectly safe to come inside. Ailsa, my third wife, wasn't one for company. She said there was always too much to do when other people came over. Since it's just me now, I find keeping house isn't such a chore, but then again I only have to keep up with myself.

After you. Turn left into the den. I left a lamp on.

Incredible, isn't it, the view from that window? Imagine the time it must have taken to place each pane within that cast iron frame. You'll most likely looking at over 100 hours of labor there. Have you counted them yet? There's 90 panes in all. I wouldn't have wanted to be one of the guys out on the scaffolding that day, lifting those things into place, miles above solid ground.

Go on, get closer. You're perfectly safe. Listen. You can still make out the neighbors' voices on the other side of the wall.

Magnificent, aren't they? Those bright lights all the way across the George Washington bridge, all the way to Jersey. Like a scene the late, great Alfred Stieglitz would have shot. I know, I know. You don't expect it, right? I was lucky. For years, the planners have been angling to put something between me and that view. Some consortium finally bought up all the land along the waterfront in the '90s. Then 9/11 happened and suddenly wealthy folk could see the benefit of low-level housing at the barricades. Game over. Go on, get closer.

Come back in daytime, and the Hudson rules, but at night electricity reigns.

You're wondering where you should sit. Take your pick. We could sit at the kitchen counter, or perhaps you'd prefer the couch.

What's that you ask?

Oh, speaking for myself, I'd only ever known 'woman' as a knot that must never be undone. For a lifetime, I have watched, with bated breath, the women who have allowed me to come closest and marveled at their dexterity to entwine with the world – be it with their children, lovers or families. As men, it can seem that we are always on the outside of something looking in.

Of course, not all men see the beauty of the knot. I've heard other men protest at woman's ways. A leash around their neck, they cry, and yet more carp about females sinking their claws into them. The latter is not a lady I know. I don't know her as owner, or beast; only as something rooted.

What's that? More light? Sure thing.

Years ago, when I was still a young guy impersonating a full-grown man, a woman I was dating asked me, acting all indignant, 'Why are you so mean to me?' And, without planning my response, I improvised, which is a sure-fire way to say the thing you really mean. My hapless response, 'Because I only know to give you what you ask for.'

Ah, reckon you don't like the sound of that much. A racist and a misogynist, no less! Well, that gives you an excuse to turn your back on me. You can tell yourself I have nothing of value to say and move on. You'll think a lot worse about me before my tale is done, no doubt. That I can accept, but passing judgment before I've got something out, now that would be cruel. I've been waiting a long time for someone to hear my story all the way to the end. Now I can't know that you're that person and you can't be sure of me, so let's make no promises, but you'll stay a while, won't you?

WALLS

SABINE MEIER

GERMANY 1961
June 15th

German Democratic Republic East Berlin,
House of Ministries, International Press Conference

There is no stopping us, radio waves, quick as light and bodiless.

We are ready, bound to carry further each sound caught by the microphone. Whether beeps and scratches, vowels and consonants, fricatives, sibilants, we will convey them all. There is no stopping us, impartial messengers, entrusted with words and their meanings, with sentences of significance, for others to decode.

The press conference begins.

Go.

Noises… Shuffling… Murmuring… Distinct words… Questions… Answers…

Nothing escapes us. Not a pause. Not a slip of the tongue. Not a single discordant note.

'Niemand hat die Absicht, eine Mauer zu errichten.'

The sentence Walter Ulbricht, head of state of the German Democratic Republic, speaks into the microphone, will be ours for a very short time.

Nobody has any intention of building a wall, Ulbricht says.

There is no stopping us. We take Ulbricht's words prisoner, make them ride up and down, up and down, in quick succession, before they stumble into an electric field and are released to those whose receivers are on the alert.

We will spread the message in Berlin.

We will spread it in East and West.

Spread it all over Germany.

All over the world.

It is nothing but another sentence, another sentence in our care.

We do not judge.

Others will.

There is no stopping us. Rushing through cloth and flesh, metal and stone, we leave behind shockwaves emanating from the journalists assembled in the great hall in the House of Ministries.

'Nobody has any intention of building a wall.'

We do not comment.

Others will.

Still indoors, we brush against painted china tiles sitting on concrete stones. A wall. Without a doubt. We do not linger, slither across the surface of the huge mural in the House of Ministries, take in beaming faces, diligent workers, obedient children, dancing pioneers, red flags in motion. A picture of a socialist state. Two-dimensional.

No time to stay.

We fly along Wilhelmstraße, flash by Humboldt-Universität, and dash along Unter den Linden. We slide through bone and brain, through clueless minds on a bus in motion.

We hurry on.

We hurry and watch. Watch citizens of East Berlin receiving the message – an elderly lady in Bernburger Straße, whose palms are pressed against a window pane, her body in the East, her glance in the West; a construction worker in Stalinallee, whose Leberwurstbrot is trapped between rotting teeth, his body turned to concrete while spit is dribbling down his chin; a medal-decorated Offizier in the Russian barracks in Berlin-Bernau, who uses his index finger to retrace the course of a wall on a map, nothing but a dark blue line on paper, top secret. His grin is a grimace of satisfaction.

A member of the Socialist Party of the GDR, who pours down a mouthful of beer, wipes his chin with the back of his hand. His radio at full volume, the communist belches, a leer on his face.

We do not comment.

Others will.

We watch – and listen.

East Berlin, a flat in the city centre

You applaud the idea of a wall. Genosse Ulbricht knows what he is doing. Good man. Excellent man. A communist. Like you. He fought on the Russian side. A partisan. He'll show them. Adenauer and Erhard. Decadent Western buggers. Fucking decadent Politiker. Keep them out of East Berlin, all of them, those Scheißkapitalisten. And the fleeing cowards attracted by the Golden West, keep them in the GDR. Make them work hard. If they give any trouble, interrogation, prison, BANG.

May a Socialist Germany flourish. Fortified, it will grow strong and resilient. Like your son. Squatting in his bed bawling. Rattling the metal netting. You have made sure he won't disturb you; you try to ignore the over-familiar wail, touch the key in your pocket. The boy had better understand that life is work and obedience.

You put up with the flat they selected for you, knowing it's temporary. Secret until that woman has given up looking for your son, your superiors say. Protected, they say. They repeat you deserve better after what you've been through. What do they know? What the hell do they know? Most of them stare at your limp. What is your injury to them? Fucking hypocrites. Soldiers don't complain. So you just smile and nod.

He is bawling again. Blubbering, squealing. Scheiße. They instructed you to keep as quiet as possible. Fuck. Fuck. Fuck. Tell a toddler to keep quiet. Scheiße, he's at it again. You grab the key; get up. You know how to make him keep his mouth shut…

West Berlin – German Democratic Republic – Helmstedt-Marienborn – Federal Republic of Germany – Braunschweig

No time to not stay. We hurry on, pass by Brandenburger Tor, reach the Western part of Berlin unnoticed. We do not need passports, cannot be stopped.

We slither along Kurfürstendamm, approach West Berliners sitting on the terrace of Café Kranzler. They have not heard. Not yet. A chubby-cheeked lady spears a slice of Schwarzwälder Kirschtorte with her fork, a frilly-aproned waitress serves a Kännchen Kaffee. We get closer. A portable radio walks past them, a hand touches a wheel, turns up the volume…

Free to do our duty, we slip through the radio's wire mesh, release the message in our care:

'Niemand hat die Absicht, eine Mauer zu errichten.'

They all listen. Not all of them understand.

A smear of whipped cream on the chubby cheek, a stain on the linen napkin, cherry red. The cup sits in a puddle of coffee. Spilt.

We do not stay.

We do not comment.

Others will.

There is no stopping us. We leave West Berlin, travel high in the air, unhindered by buildings, people, ideologies. Unhindered by borders. We fly across the German Democratic Republic until we reach Grenzübergang Helmstedt-Marienborn.

In the West again, we hurry on until we reach Braunschweig, about 200 km from where the press conference is still in progress. And here, too, we will release our message wherever a receiver is on the alert.

Braunschweig listens and watches.

In Leisewitzstraße a sour-faced primary school teacher takes a break from marking dictations; in Böcklerstraße a single mother struggles to answer her daughter's questions; one floor below, a retired professor of English tries to forget about his failed efforts to write a poem.

They all listen.

We do not comment.

These people will.

Federal Republic of Germany
Braunschweig, Leisewitzstraße 7

She put her palms to her cheeks, unable to sit still. On the television screen, grey and black hazes moved unsteadily across Ulbricht's bearded face. Melitta Kirchhoff bent forward. Her hands gripped the armrests. A press conference in East Berlin. She prised her hands from the wood, blood puckering under the skin of her palms. She did not feel pain, just watched and listened. East Berlin. Dozens of reporters, tense, their faces serious, their mouths lines of anxiety. Then Ulbricht spoke, his tone evasive, his eyes shifty...

'Niemand hat die Absicht, eine Mauer zu errichten.'

What? That was... Ulbricht was lying, like a snotty-nosed first year. Melitta knew. She just knew. What a cheek. What a ridiculous charade. Ha. The Staatsratsvorsitzende of the GDR was lying, had just blabbed a secret. Ha. A wall would keep people from leaving East Berlin, so close to the western part of the city, too close to capitalist Germany.

Melitta had to think. Urgently. At the moment, there were regular trains from Braunschweig to West Berlin. Access to the Eastern part of the city was easy. Easy. Now.

Melitta struggled to keep her composure and shivered. This was her last chance. She pressed her lips shut, hearing without listening, looking without seeing. Jarring, distorted sounds echoed through her living room. Hues of black and white. And somewhere in between – grey. That was life.

She switched off the TV, stared at the screen until nothing remained but a milky grey pane of glass. And in that pane, misted over by memories, she saw him. The man who lived in East Berlin, the man she hated – and feared. Melitta stood up abruptly and yanked open a window, her hands wandering to her cheeks again. In spite of the summery air, her skin felt chilly.

Cold. He was cold and hard. He had hurt her, sneering. Back then. If she wanted to find him, if she wanted to pay him back in kind, she would have to do it soon, very soon – before they built that wall. She would have to be colder and harder than him. And more cunning.

She closed her eyes. Saw him, smelt him, felt him, feared

him, all over again. Could she find him? Lash out at him to finally stop herself from seeing, feeling, fearing him, all over again? Could she?

Her cheeks were hot to the touch in the chilling breeze from East Berlin.

Twenty-three corrected dictations later, she had made a decision. She would not lose her grip. Not at school and not anywhere else. Melitta Kirchhoff never gave up, whatever the cost. Accounts were best settled before the wall was erected. Yes. Oh yes.

Braunschweig, Böcklerstr. 2a, first floor

'Mutti, they won't build a wall all across Berlin, will they?' Hannah asked.

'Hannah, I don't know.'

Mutti didn't even turn her head towards her. She was sitting on the edge of the armchair and didn't move, not a bit – as if she'd forgotten her own body, or switched it off somehow. Except for her ears. They stuck out like two red antennae. And although Mutti had been listening closely, she couldn't answer Hannah's question.

Adults often said they knew everything – but they didn't. Like Albrecht Zander, who hadn't even read the stories by Enid Blyton even though he'd been a professor of English, before he got old. Professors at university were like teachers at school – kind of.

Hannah loved school. There were ice cream classes and cauliflower classes. Funny that, ice cream classes never lasted long enough, and made her feel nice all over her body. Cauliflower classes made her feel sad and grumpy at the same time. She hated cauliflower. Ugh. Fräulein Kirchhoff was a cauliflower teacher. Tomorrow she'd ask the class about Berlin and about that wall. And she'd expect an answer. Hadn't the crackly old voice said that nobody wanted to build a wall?

'Mutti, didn't the man say…'

'Shush, Hannah.'

The ears were still glowing. Hannah would have liked to touch them to feel if they were as hot as they looked – but she knew Mutti wouldn't let her because she was a big girl now. Hannah didn't want to be a big girl if that meant she had to be quiet when she needed an adult to explain to her what was going on.

Fizz-bzzt… Another, younger voice – Crackleman had stopped speaking – screeched its way into their living room… buzzzzz-fizz-eeeeh-bzzt… Hannah covered her ears.

'Muttiiiiii!'

Her mother looked as if she'd just woken up. Hannah knew because Mutti's eyes were somehow turned inwards. Mutti rushed over to the radio, squatted down in front of it, and turned the big wheel – buzzzzz-fizz-eeeeh-bzzt… Crouching next to her, and keeping her hands pressed against her ears, Hannah saw the needle tremble a little – and then the younger voice was back.

'Bztt-fizz-eeeh-ker-ching... Allied Forces... eeeh-cracklebzzt... protect the sovereign rights of... bzzt... determined to... buzzscreeech...

'Muttiii, turn it off. Pleeaase.'

As if someone had told the voice to be quiet, it got slower... and slower... rumm... ble... groa... groannnnnn... groagroannn... and then it stopped. Phew.

Mutti made a strange sound, a mixture between a hiccup and a sob, got up from the floor, and gave Hannah a big cuddle. But when Hannah saw her mother's eyes, she knew something was very, very wrong because they looked like liquid marbles again, for the first time in ages. Hannah had seen Mutti's marble eyes so often when Vater was still at home. She was really glad her mother didn't want Vater back – but they both missed Max, her baby brother.

Mutti took her hand, went over to the sofa, and patted the seat next to her.

'Sit down, Hannah. We have to talk.'

*

Karin had rarely felt so helpless. Could she saddle Hannah with the truth, the child who had been beaten by her stepfather Robert with a belt – and had not told Karin about it? Would Hannah understand what a wall in Berlin meant? Karin turned towards her daughter. Hannah was quicker.

'You tell me I'm a big girl now, Mutti.'

Karin did not speak. She just put her arm around her daughter, too raw to trust her voice.

'And big girls need to know what's going on,' Hannah added.

Karin could not stop a tear from running down her own cheek. What a snivelling coward, what a miserable mother she was. She wiped the tear away. Hannah's face crumpled. And yet her daughter did not cry, but swallowed. Swallowed hard. So much resilience in such a slender body. Hannah was a fighter. Karin took a deep breath. Yes, they would fight. Mother and daughter. Together. Dry-eyed.

'Ouch,' Hannah said.

Karin loosened her grip. Her closest ally was only eight years old.

'Hannah, darling, you know that Vater left for East Berlin and took Max with him.'

Her daughter did not smile, just nodded, but snuggled closer to her.

'On the radio we heard that they might possibly build a wall between East and West Berlin,' Karin added.

'Didn't the old man on the radio say they wouldn't do it?'

Her clever daughter.

'Yes, Hannah, but sometimes people say a thing and everybody feels they mean the opposite.'

'I know, Mutti.'

Karin would have expected disbelief and further questions. Her daughter's reaction left her speechless. What did an eight-year-old child know about hypocrisy and deception?

'We have a teacher...'

Hannah interrupted herself and turned her head away.

'What do you mean, Hannah?'

'Nothing.'

Clammed up. Further questions useless. For now.

'Can't we travel to Berlin and go and fetch Max?' Hannah said.

Trust Hannah to read her thoughts.

'Yes, Hannah, we will try – you and me together – before they can build a wall.'

Hannah's eyes glowed with anticipation. Karin would not dampen her childlike enthusiasm. The danger of failing was immense. But try they would.

Braunschweig, Böcklerstr. 2a, ground floor

A short snapping noise...

Albrecht flinched. His glasses slid down his nose. He pushed them up, and stared at the splintered wood, at the hole distorting the word he had just written. A word he had struggled with. Too much pressure. The tip of the pencil lead stuck out at an awkward angle, like a broken bone. When he raised his hand to have a closer look, the leaden limb fell off. Amputated. How suitable. The mutilated word had been a bad choice anyway, its metaphorical value lacking. Was für ein Trauerspiel.

He dropped the pencil. It jumped up, quivered, and came

to a halt in the middle of Notebook No 97. Listless. Albrecht got up from his chair. It creaked. So did his knees. Body and mind bruised. Time for restorative action. He walked briskly over to the shelves and switched on the radio. Distraction. He turned the knob until the needle found its habitual place. Norddeutscher Rundfunk, his favourite radio station. A crackling noise. Someone was speaking into a microphone. He forced himself to concentrate on the voice. A female reporter from the Frankfurter Rundschau asking a question. The news, obviously. Good.

'Ich verstehe Ihre Frage so...'

That must be... that was Walter Ulbricht's voice. Unmistakable. The Staatsratsvorsitzende was answering the reporter's question. How annoying Albrecht had not listened properly before. He would now.

'... Menschen in Westdeutschland gibt, die wünschen, dass wir die Bauarbeiter in der Hauptsstadt der DDR mobilisieren, um eine Mauer aufzurichten...'

What? A wall? Ulbricht was talking about a wall. In Berlin. Albrecht grabbed the shelf in front of him for support. But... what Ulbricht had just said was nonsense. Of course people in Western Germany did not want a wall to be built. Utter nonsense. The man was prevaricating. A poor orator indeed. A demented fantasist. A communist. A puppet on Russian...

'Niemand hat die Absicht eine Mauer zu errichten.'

Albrecht gasped. Could it be true? Would a wall separate the East from the West? He felt his knees tremble.

His beloved Berlin. His youth. His youth walled off from his life? He took two shaky steps across the room and flopped into an armchair.

He closed his eyes, did not hear the radio any more. He just heard his thoughts –

galloping, hurdling… bolting.

When would that gottverdammte wall be built? He would be too late, had left it too long. He made a fist and pounded it against the armrest. Thump.

His knuckles hurt. He did not mind the pain.

He needed to make an appointment with his university friend Kurt Böning in East Berlin. Urgently. Thump.

The capital would be divided into freedom – and oppression. Thump.

The GDR must be desperate to prevent more and more Germans from leaving for the West. Thump.

He stared at his reddened knuckles, pressed them to his lips. The economy of the Bundesrepublik was thriving – in the GDR basic food was rationed. Marktwirtschaft versus Planwirtschaft. How would the government of the Bundesrepublik Deutschland react, how America, how Great Britain, how France?

Kalter Krieg.

Albrecht shuddered. Was im Himmel was he supposed to do?

INTERFERENCE

SUSAN ALLOTT

Interference is set between England and Australia, exploring the long and complex relationship between these nations, using a modern-day plot set in 1997 and a backstory set in 1967. Isla Green, the protagonist, is four years old when her mother clears out the savings account and takes her home to England, leaving her dad, Joe, in the turbulent company of bored, sensual Mandy.

Mandy's husband Steve is a policeman whose job involves removing indigenous children from their families. He is very much in love with his wife and wants to start a family. Unknown to him, Mandy is still taking the pill. Believing they can't have children, he brings an indigenous baby home and persuades Mandy they should raise the child as their own.

Joe's affair with Mandy starts as a distraction but quickly gets serious. When Steve finds out and leaves her, taking the baby with him, Mandy decides she wants to save her marriage. Joe is not prepared to let her go.

When Isla and her mum return to Sydney, Mandy and Steve's house is empty. As an adult, Isla discovers they did not move away as a couple. Nobody seems to know where Mandy went, or where she is now. Her dad claims he doesn't know either. Is he the great guy Isla believes him to be? Or is he hiding something?

Ivanhoe, New South Wales, 1967

Steve saw her first, kneeling in the dirt at the edge of the creek. She looked happy enough. Five or six mates with her, poking at something in the water with a stick. He looked away, kept his foot on the gas and hoped to God she'd run off before Harry spotted her. His shirt was wet against the car seat. He hummed a tune, to break the silence, and let himself believe he wouldn't have to do this one; he'd tell Ray they couldn't find her. With any luck they'd have a busy few months and it would go on the back burner. He'd be able to sleep tonight.

No such luck. The kid jumped to her feet and started shouting at the others to come and see, come and look at this. Waving the bloody stick in the air. Steve kept driving, kept humming, and she kept waving the stick and yelling. What did she have to go and do that for?

'There she is!' Harry jumped clean out of his seat. 'Over there, by the creek.'

Steve braked. Turned off the ignition. 'Well spotted, mate.'

Harry wandered over to her, nice and easy, for all the world like he was her favourite uncle come to visit. He started talking to her, squatting down by the water. Steve knew what he'd say: 'I'm going to take you for a ride in a police truck.' He always said that. 'And then you're going to have a little holiday.'

Steve climbed out of the truck and waited. Harry held his hand out and the girl took it. She was taken with him, you could see it. Looking up at him and smiling. With any luck they could do this nice and quick without a scene.

'There's a baby too,' Harry said, just loud enough to reach him. 'A boy.'

'Do we need to do that today?'

'I should say we do.' Harry looked at him like he was out of his mind. 'Get the job done, mate. No sense dragging it out.'

He held the door open for the kid and she got in and knelt on the back seat. 'Where am I going on holiday?' She was looking wary. 'Can I say goodbye to Grandpa?'

'I'll speak to him,' Steve said. His voice sounded fake, like an actor with a bit part. 'I'll let him know.'

'Get a bloody move on,' said Harry, still with the nice guy smile on his face. 'And don't let 'em get to you. It's been signed off.'

The house was quiet. Tin-roof veranda and a dog sleeping in the shade. He knocked, not too loud, but footsteps came right away. He braced himself. No going back now.

'What's wrong?' An old fella answered the door. Full

blood Aboriginal. Darker than the girl. Black skin and white hair, like a photo negative. He was none too happy to see a copper on the doorstep, and he'd clocked the truck down by the creek too. 'What's the problem?'

A baby cried quietly in the front room, out of sight. Beside him, the dog was on its feet, baring its teeth, snarling.

'I'm here about the kids,' Steve said. 'You the grandpa?'

'What d'you mean?' He took a better look at the truck and saw Dora in the back seat. He reared back in shock. Tried to push past, hollering her name.

'Listen. Don't make this hard on yourself.' Steve held him by the shoulder, gripped him there and shoved him back into the house, just enough force so he knew this was serious. He was a nasty bastard when he needed to be. 'Let me in.'

It was dark inside, and a tight knot of flies was frantic over a piece of meat he'd got on a plate near the stove. Three empty beer bottles lined up next to the sink. The baby had gone quiet, propped up on the couch in a singlet and a nappy. Big wet eyes following him as he moved.

'Where's the mother?'

'Out,' the old fella said, and looked at his feet. 'Her sisters help with the kids.' He stepped closer to the baby. 'There's three sisters and five cousins. Plenty of us to care for the young'uns.'

'Look, mate. We've been told to take the baby. Orders from above.'

The old fella shook his head. 'You can't take him.' He

picked the boy up and held him tight, both arms across his body. 'We're a loving family. We look after the kids.'

A fly circled the room, thumped against the small window and dropped to the floor. The room was stifling. Steve started feeling separate from his body, like he might not be in charge of himself. He didn't know what he'd do next. The baby turned to him with a steady gaze, wise and sad, like he knew how this was going to play out. He locked eyes with the baby and tried to move.

'I'm not going to take him,' he said. 'You get to keep the boy.' The old bloke didn't react. Steve didn't know if he'd said what he thought he'd said. 'I'm going to leave him here with you. I won't take him.'

The old man started to cry then. No warning. Started bawling and shaking his head, rocking the baby side to side. He knew what was coming.

'What about Dora?'

'She's coming with me, mate. Foster family's lined up already.' He went into automatic; the usual old bull. 'She'll be looked after. She'll get a good education. Good start in life.'

He cried silently, his face stretched long and trembling. 'Can I see her?'

'Best you don't. Stay here and keep the baby quiet. I'll have to take him else.'

Steve heard the old man wailing as he shut the door behind him. White, hard sunlight after the dark of the house. The dog lifted its head and got up on its haunches, barked at him 'til he was off the property.

He shook his head at Harry as he got into the truck.

'No baby in there,' he told him. His hand trembled on the ignition. He wanted to cry himself, now he was out of there, away from the old man and his fear, his grief. He had no reason to cry next to that, but still his throat ached and his eyes threatened to well up. He was a lily livered, poisonous bastard. He couldn't even look at the girl in the back.

'Your grandpa says to be a good girl.' He said it without turning. 'He says to sit down nice and quiet and don't muck about.'

He reversed back a few yards and a great cloud of dust rose up around them.

The old bloke was out on the veranda as he pulled away. He was chasing the truck. Steve crunched through the gears, put his foot down and drove blind through the dust 'til he'd gone.

Sydney, New South Wales, 1967

Mandy had taken her eye off of Isla for one minute. Two minutes, maximum. She'd been right there in the wet sand, a few feet away, digging a hole with her hands. Mandy stood beside the little hole Isla had dug; the damp heaps of sand beside it. The hole was full of water. A huge great wave had come and covered the beach, wetting the tip of Mandy's towel. Which was when she'd looked up and found Isla gone.

She searched up and down the beach; strode off in one direction shouting Isla's name, then went back the way she came and did the same thing. She must have missed her. She kept looking, kept calling. There were too many little girls in blue swimmers on this beach. All of them looked familiar from a distance and became strangers as she drew closer. She let panic seize her. She stood on the shingle and faced out to the water, calling again, her voice lost among the boom and crash of the waves. The heat of the day, the laughter and movement, became nauseating; the gulls sounded shrill and full of dread. She waded into the sea, at a loss, and shouted: 'Isla! Isla!'

The waves were coming in tall and strong. She tried to head back to shore but a wave rose up and she was caught in the swell, lifted off her feet and carried powerfully to the beach, where she landed on her forearms, imagining Isla drowned, her neck broken, her lungs full of water.

She pulled herself to her knees, hooking the straps of her costume back over her shoulders, coughing. Further down the beach, Isla waved, and ran towards her through the shallows.

'Mandy!' Isla was wearing red swimmers. Red. 'I saw you in the water! You got your hair wet!'

This was why Mandy didn't have children. It was scary, and exhausting. She crawled onto the beach where their towels were laid out and sat herself down. Christ Almighty.

'You went swimming!' Isla landed on her knees in the sand. 'Did you like it?'

'Not much.' Mandy laughed. It was time to hand this child back to her mother. She pushed Isla's flattened, gritty hair out of her face. 'I didn't see that wave coming.'

'You said you hate the water.'

'I do!' Mandy pulled her costume away from her skin and saw she had sand all over the place, thickly gathered in the folds of her belly. 'Let's go and get showered. Your mum will be back soon. We should head home.'

Isla shook her head. 'She won't be back yet. She went shopping. I reckon she'll be ages.'

'It's getting choppy out there. That's enough for today.' She stood, and reached for her towel, flicking the worst of the sand out of it. 'Tell you what. Next time we'll catch a shark and take it home for lunch. How's that sound?'

Isla nodded, and picked up her own towel. 'Tomorrow, can we?'

'Don't see why not.' She nodded up at the showers at the top of the beach. 'You have first shower. I'll be right behind you.'

Mandy's legs were heavy as she followed Isla up the coastal path towards the house. She stood a moment under the shade of the gum trees, listening to the waves, getting her breath back. Steve would be back soon. He'd been away a full week, so he must have finished the job. She had a bad feeling about this one, she didn't know why. It was getting harder for him as time went on. And it was getting harder to deal with him afterwards.

Her skin turned cold, thinking of it. She found her sundress, sandy and damp at the bottom of her bag, and pulled it over her head, brushed the dried sand from her skin and climbed the last few yards to the bottom of her backyard. The best she could hope for was that he wouldn't get back before she'd had a chance to open the gin.

'Mummy's back already!' Isla ran across the yard towards her. 'She's back! She didn't even get any shopping!' Isla stopped and attempted a handstand, leaving one foot on the grass, one bent leg pointing skywards. She stood back up and lifted her hands above her head, triumphant. 'That's why she's cranky, and much too hot.'

Mandy followed Isla across the grass to where Louisa was waiting for them at the back of the house. She looked gorgeous, as usual. Tall and elegant in a pale blue dress, perfectly upright, and that dark slab of hair down her back. Mandy felt plump and crumpled in her presence.

'You should have let yourself in, Lou. Door's open.'

'I've only been waiting a few minutes.' Louisa held her arm across her forehead to block the sun. 'I was quicker than I expected. Thanks for having her.'

'Don't mention it. We had a great time.' Mandy pushed the back door open, dropped her bag down on the lino and switched the electric fan on, more for Louisa's benefit than her own. 'Come in and I'll fix you a drink. You look like you need a pick me up. I know I do.'

Louisa picked up a coaster and fanned herself. 'Sounds wonderful.'

She seemed nervy, smiling too brightly, Mandy thought.

She tried to catch her eye, but Louisa sat down at the kitchen table and stared out at the yard, kicking her long legs out in front of her. The sun was pulling back behind the house, and Isla was skipping up and down, her shadow folding over the plant pots and the coil of garden hose.

'Is anything wrong?'

Louisa turned back to face her. The smile had gone. 'I made a down payment,' she said, waving a fly away. 'I went into town to make a down payment.'

'On what?'

She glanced out at Isla in the yard. 'Fix me that drink and I'll tell you.'

Mandy flexed the ice tray and dropped a few cubes into each tumbler. 'Happy new year, Lou.' She knocked her glass against Louisa's. 'Here's to 1967.'

'You got a new watch?' Louisa reached for the Timex, which sat on the kitchen table, curled around the salt and pepper.

'Got it for Christmas.'

'It's beautiful.'

'D'you think?' The alcohol had gone to Mandy's head already. 'I can't get used to it. Never had a watch before.'

Louisa wrapped it around her own wrist and fastened the buckle. She stretched her arm out to look at it, turning it back and forth. Her arm was damp with a fine sheen of sweat, Mandy noticed. Even her sweat was lovely. And the watch suited her, of course.

'You should wear it,' Louisa said. 'It's elegant.'

Mandy smiled, and took the watch from Louisa. 'That's the problem,' she said. 'I'm not the elegant sort.'

Out in the yard, Isla yelped and ran across the flagstones, laughing. She'd disturbed a lizard, most likely. She liked to creep up and prod them with the hose.

Mandy buckled the watch, keeping it loose so it didn't pinch. She'd been about to say something, but it had gone. No matter. Louisa sat back and lifted her hair, pulling it into a comb. Lou was always too hot, always fanning herself and looking for the shade. Sometimes she reminded Mandy of her mother; just the British accent and the way she missed home. Her mum had never let up about the stinking heat, as she'd called it. Nothing had cheered her up like a dark bank of cloud.

'What did you say about a down payment, Lou?'

'Isla, don't run!' Louisa sighed as Isla bolted past them, straight through the kitchen into the living room. 'Slow down!'

Isla jumped onto the couch to look out of the window. Mandy took a gulp of gin and waited. Isla must have heard Steve's truck from the yard.

'Steve's back!' Isla held on to the back of the couch and sprang up and down, her backside in the air. 'He's back, Mandy!'

Mandy stood at the window and looked out. Steve was parked up already, and the truck was filthy, as always. Mud-caked wheels; brick red dust at the fenders. The windscreen was covered in muck but for the small double-arc of the wipers.

Steve turned the engine off and slumped over the steering

wheel, resting his head on the bridge of his hands.

Mandy's stomach turned. 'Here we go,' she said, as he lifted his head. She stepped away from the window, afraid to catch his eye.

'Here we go!' Isla leapt off the couch and turned a pirouette. 'Here we go!'

'Isla, stop jumping around.' Louisa stood in the doorway with Isla's sandals in one hand. 'We should get going.'

'No rush. Don't feel you have to leave.'

'No, we'll be off. Steve will want a bit of quiet, if he's been away.'

Mandy nodded and stubbed her cigarette out in the ashtray on the coffee table. She could see from here, he wasn't going to keep it together on account of company.

'I hope he's not too cut up, this time. It's a tough old job. And he takes it hard.'

Louisa looked blankly back at her. Sometimes people didn't listen, Mandy thought, when you told them your darkest secrets. Or they managed not to hold on to what they heard. They let themselves forget.

IN CONTROL

JOSE VARGHESE

Rhonda felt dizzy as she huddled with the other passengers on the aerobridge. She felt unwell. Another attack of tinnitus, or was there something really strange about the air?

It was odd that a large number of the airport crew lined up on both sides as if they were escorting the passengers to a specific place. They wore uniforms that looked odd. Somewhat like overalls, silver in colour, covering their whole body except for the eyes and nose. The logos on their chests and arms were indecipherable.

'Are we really in Gatwick, or are we hijacked and have ended up in some godforsaken-fundamentalist-nowhere?' said the cheeky middle-aged man. He had been sitting next to her and sleeping through the entire flight.

'Looks like we made a mistake,' he mumbled, pretending horror.

'No way! Didn't you hear the announcements as we landed? We are in Gatwick, trust me!' Rhonda gave him a reassuring wink.

She too was dead asleep when they landed, though. Did she hear the announcements?

One look towards the left as they moved out of the bridge, and she knew there was indeed something wrong. She saw through the glass wall a few passengers at the waiting area. They wore strange clothes too – identical cloaks in various colours that reduced each one of them to a shapeless mass. To add to it, they all looked weird for some reason. She couldn't pin it down, but they looked much less energetic than normal people; even a bit lifeless.

It appalled her that their lifelessness was thanks to the overt lack of 'normal' communication among them. There were people sitting on sofas, looking at one another, their facial expressions changing once in a while, a nod of yes or no in between, and they generally acted as if they were talking among themselves through some strange device. But she couldn't find anything attached to their ears or any other part of their body. Their fingers weren't busy texting. Their hands rested motionless on their laps like stuffed squirrels that won't impress an onlooker beyond a point. Then she noticed that none of those people were holding a mobile phone or tablet either.

'Now that's really strange!' she said.

'What?' the middle-aged man asked.

'I mean, look at those people... none of them are using a mobile phone! I never thought I would witness something like this in my lifetime!'

'You are right. And I am still not convinced that we are in the right place, or at the right time.'

'But, if you forgive the cliché, don't they say that we are in the only place and at the only time we have?'

'Well, I really doubt that now, young lady...'

Rhonda didn't realise then that this was the last bit of conventional conversation she would have with someone, in what was left of her life.

*

There were a large number of checkout counters and each had just two or three passengers lined up in front of them. No computer screens, no cameras, no scanning machines, no rubber stamps. The young man at her counter just kept staring at her eyes and dissuaded her, non-verbally, from any attempt at speaking. She had no choice but to stare back.

And that's when it happened. She started to receive some signals through a device they fixed on her head; something like thought-waves. They didn't really make much sense at first. She tried to focus intently. There seemed to be no other choice.

By the time she could decipher something from the signals, she was too exhausted to realise how shocking its content was.

/ You are dead, for three years / – the signal said.

/ Oh, that's funny! / – a message went out from her brain.

There was no expression in the eyes of the young man. But he didn't stop staring.

/ Don't worry, though. It's all right. / – Another thought-wave from him.

/ What's all right? That I am dead? That I have to stand here like a fool staring at your dead face? / – she thought-waved back.

/ I'm afraid you have to calm down, madam. High thought-frequencies in an animated fashion can damage our communication channel. /

Calm down...

She had to find a way out of the situation, even if it meant obeying the commands of an uninspiring twenty-something 'waving' stupid thoughts at her face – like she was already dead.

/ Okay. Tell me in clear terms what you mean, then. /

/ I will. You are Rhonda Stevenson, 32 years old when you boarded the plane on February 12th, 2018. You might not have realised it, but there was an accident while the flight disappeared for a period from our tracking system. Your flight passed through a zone that shifted you to a state where there was an issue with the relativity of time. /

/ Stop giving me an SF plot, man! Come to the point. /

/ Well, I'll spare you the details, because you aren't going to grasp it anyway. You have landed properly in Gatwick, but this accident has transported you to the future – fifteen years, to be precise. /

/ What the he... /

/ Hang on, Rhonda. Let me finish. The present date is March 26th, 2033. What's even more remarkable in your case is that our records show that you died on March 3rd, 2030. /

/ Are you kidding me? So, where am I now – at the pearly gates after three years of post-mortem limbo? And who are you – a silly Peter in glasses? /

/ Sorry madam, you aren't allowed to speak in those terms anymore. We have strictly kept any religious terminology out of our system, in favour of reasoning. Objective analyses of… /

/ Oh, no! Where have I landed? /

/ You are all right madam. It's only that we have a unique situation with this flight's arrival. But it's not only you – there are a hundred and eighty-three people, including the passengers and the crew. All of your bodies have not aged or undergone any observable change while you passed through the zone, but our database has an entirely different set of information for these fifteen years in between. We need to make certain arrangements, especially in the case of twenty-one people among you who are shown as dead in our records. /

/And what would that be? /

/ You have to be isolated. Some sort of rehabilitation. /

/ See, you need to explain this. What's the crime I committed? And, how can your records show that I am dead three years back when I was not even around? /

/ You are right to feel that way Rhonda. But our records are based on fool-proof data. What was known as predictive medical research and preventive treatment in your time had progressed dramatically – and we can now have accurate findings on the death date of any individual from sample analyses of your cells, which was done at the gate before you entered here. /

/ Oh, so that was all the fuss? What else have you found out about me then, other than the fact that my existence is an illusion? /

/ Pretty much everything, madam. Though we don't have the data for the work you could have individually done in the fifteen years that lapsed, our analyses show that your work output in your field – architectural engineering – prior to your flight was less than thirty percent of your potential. /

/ Are you kidding me? How can you make such a judgement, sitting there? I can't allow you to say such irresponsible things to my face, while I know for sure how dedicated I had… /

/ Wait, madam. Perhaps a good enough percentage in your time, when you compared it with the performance of your peers. But in today's world, we are trying to extract the maximum potential of each individual; at least a ninety percent. /

/ You are confusing me. /

/ Listen, we have a certain system which allots an ideal number of hours that's needed in an individual's lifetime for what we call 'essential distractions' – like interpersonal relations, expressions of physical togetherness, the reproductive process, interference with the raising of the next generation and so on. By minimising all this to a total of five years in someone's adult life, we zero in on what one could contribute to the future and well-being of the planet we live in. /

/ Oh, really? /

/ We have more or less eradicated the entertainment aspect from human life – no mass production of art or literature now. Communication is strictly monitored, to channelize it to the informative aspect. The concept of family or other social institutions don't exist now. Romantic relationships between people are not allowed. Physical activities are also restricted in order to… /

/ I'm sorry, but that's all I can take at one go. So, you mean I have landed in a different world with nothing to relate to my times other than my memories? /

/ I'm afraid we have to erase that as well, so as to make the best use of the twelve years you can live here, though in isolation. But it's for your good, because we will program you for the rest of your life with the help of a couple more implants. You will get the best medical care and you won't have to go through any emotional trauma related to physical illnesses or troubled relationships, which were the major reasons for your under-performance in your previous life. /

/ So, you are going to finish me off? /

/ What do you mean, madam? We're not going to finish you off, but we're giving you a new life, with the maximum productivity that you can… /

/ I find no meaning in all that. If you take away my memories, I am dead. /

/ Please don't see it that way. Once you are reprogrammed for… /

/ How long do I have, to retain my memories? /

/ A minimum of five minutes from now, or a maximum of twenty-four hours during which you will stay isolated, as for the rest of your life. /

/ Can I be in touch with Liza? /

/ Your daughter? You can't meet her, because she is not the 11-year-old you left behind, but 26 now, an adult like you. And, no human being can be in direct touch with you now – it's against our clearly defined ethics. But, if it's your last wish from your previous life, we can arrange a ten-minute thought-wave session, provided Liza agrees to that. /

*

The white spotless walls surrounding her in the isolation home were unsettling. There was no means at all for recreation, or even to engage with herself. Every second of her activity was monitored. She felt like shouting out her thoughts, so that the idiots get to know what they have done to her? But then, the chilling realization that she didn't have to do that dawned on her. Her mind was no more her private property because of the partial implant in her brain. Anyone could access her mind, and though she herself couldn't be in control of the thoughts that took shape there, others could analyse their potential.

She longed for some music. Or a pen and a piece of paper, or even the phone they had confiscated. She could have given vent to her thoughts in an organized way, just for herself, and looked at them, old-world style, to discover a bit of herself before she gave away her life. Could it be better or worse than what she had understood as death?

The best thing to do was to focus on the thought-wave session. It was tough to adjust the time frame – she left Liza at her sister Rachel's place just five days back before flying to Berlin, and now she had to prepare for communication with a grown-up daughter who might see Rhonda as her long-lost mother. She had no idea what she would tell Liza in ten minutes, but she began to lose herself in an imaginary monologue, even as she kept looking at the communication box on which a green light would blink when/if Liza was ready for the thought-wave session.

Liza… where are you now? What have come of your fears, of your frail heart? I left you a fragile being, a weak girl. Did I even know that I wouldn't come back for the next fifteen years?

How did you cope with a tough life till the day they decided our responses to life situations didn't really matter? Would you decide to take their offer of temporarily reinstalling the memory-chip of your life lived with me? How much would it cost your career in astrophysics? A total of one hour taken away from it for analysing our lost life and a ten-minute thought-wave session with your hapless mother?

Would you forgive me for my bad decision, to fly away for the conference at which I could meet my old professors and colleagues? It was to keep our doors open to the wide world darling, for the two of us to stay in comfortable homes, and not to worry too much about mortgages.

Did you resent my image of a career woman who cost you a father? Would you ever understand why Jim had never been as good a husband to me as he had been a father to you? Would you forgive me for keeping my options open, to find someone, something, to fill the void Jim left in our life?

Rhonda felt she could go on forever. Did it mean that her life was to revolve around Liza if the accident hadn't taken place? Was that silly guy at the airport counter right about the productivity theory? Rhonda wondered whether her previous life would have been less fulfilled if she continued getting entangled in relationships even as she was obsessed with the little life of Liza she felt she had the responsibility to mould. Was she doomed that way? Is there some hope now?

Ronda felt Liza could be better off in the new life. Well, it's her only life, since she didn't miss a train like Rhonda. It must have been a smooth transformation, as all the research in the direction of making human lives more meaningful could have assisted her.

Could she have managed to shed her dependence on me? The data shows that she would have a longer life than me – she would live till her late sixties, with that weak heart and fragility that gave me sleepless nights. Perhaps they are right - we could have saved a lot of our time, or even used it proactively, if we knew a bit of what the future held in store.

Rhonda's fingers tingled. She remembered the people in the airport waiting room, their hands like stuffed squirrels, their mouths shut tight. The pleasures of communication derived from her mouth and fingers were to be history now. The thought-waves that go directly to her brain can be controlled in better ways once they were done with the programming and implants. She would overcome the obstacle of languages as well. Languages were dead.

/ It's a pre-Babel world we've reclaimed. We can communicate through thought-waves, in any part of the world. /

That's what the young man at the airport counter said.

She should have asked him his name, of course through a thought-wave. But she was annoyed that he kept stuffing so much information down her throat. And he kept 'madam-ing' her, as if she were ancient!

Rhonda didn't want to think of Jim. He had damaged her self-esteem when she was still too young. What the new people call 'expressions of physical togetherness', and was referred to as 'sex' in her time, hadn't worked out well in her life. Did it matter that it wasn't entirely the fault of her partners? Should she tell Liza her secret, that she is… was… a lesbian?

Did such categorizations mean anything in Liza's life? All the social conditioning, repressions, judgements of a world that made life difficult for anyone who didn't confirm to norms? All that identity politics that confounded an individual's quest for self-expression? All those organizations which had a hidden agenda as much as representative figures who had individual interests? Had life been easy either way?

Rhonda hoped Liza was better off, that she had used, or would use, her five years of personal relationships in a much better way, so as to go back to what she was best with a perfect conviction of the economy of movement.

What about memories?

*

'Trust me Liza, it will go away...' Rhonda would tell Liza whenever a nightmare woke her.

She would nestle her in her bosom and feel her hair. The faint heartbeat of the girl would both scare and reassure her. She tried all that she could do to keep Liza away from trouble. And just one nightmare a week was enough to ruin them all. Rhonda wished she could cast a spell over the girl's mind.

She would make hand gestures like a magician.

'Liza, your mind is in your control now. No more nightmares. You can control your dreams...'

Liza would give her a weak smile, knowing that it was all make-believe.

*

Rhonda ran towards the communication box when the green light blinked. She couldn't help holding her stifled words.

'Liza... my baby... I'm sorry, I'm so sorry... Did you miss mamma?'

They ricocheted. The box beeped, showing some error.

There was no response for a while, then the green light flickered.

She began to receive the first thought-waves from Liza.

/ Rhonda, be a brave woman. Things have changed. It's not going to be easy, but trust me, it will work. You can be in control of your thoughts soon. /

WRITER

JAX BURGOYNE

A man makes a wish on a typewriter to be rid of memories of a woman. At first happy, he then falls in love with a woman who points out that she could be her. Against at first taunts and then threats from the typewriter, he tries to find a way to ensure that he never 're-eats his own vomit'. But his life is being written. Possibly. He gives up on his hopefully new love repeatedly, but is drawn ever back to her. Finally, he learns a magic he believes darker than the 'writer – that will enable him to see one glimpse of his woman from the past.

What he sees is his daughter, who died. So he watches her life as he bleeds to death.

PROLOGUE

Someone is walking under a black sky towards a house. A white house, wooden slats, blue grey on the lintels and window frames, on the doors, the shutters, overhang of the roof. The roof is slate.

The house is preserved like it's fresh-made, but the garden is tangled like uncivilised hair. It wants to go everywhere, but somehow it stops at the house. Everything else is full of wild roses and ground elder and poison ivy and blackberry bushes with rejected black clusters.

The garden stops at the house, and at the gate, and there are invisible walls along the channel between these two things – the path to the door – which is kept sterile and ready (clear).

It is not night; it is dawn. The darkness is from a storm ready to come.

The woman has hidden her face under a veil. She is dressed for church, and a large cross balances itself on her protruding belly – she is pregnant. She pauses at the gate – looks left, right, and behind her. Then pauses some more, her hand on the latch. She is pouring some courage into herself: this is an act of will.

Once she has sufficient, she walks along the clear path with the Southern jungle holding itself – or being held – leaves parallel with the top of her hat, excited. An unseen gardener has come and not cut and trimmed the plants to keep the path clear; instead he (it) has carefully turned around every tendril that went forward or, rather, simply disallowed it.

Her hat is black and has a crow's feather pierced into it for decoration, and it should be clarified that she is dressed in black: for that other side of church business.

So she is Moses, the plants held parted for her, as she walks through the blackberries, and then she enters the house, mounts the stairs, mounts another, smaller set of stairs, opens the door, and enters the attic.

She looks up, at the open window. Her breathing is hard here, the air refusing, but she remembers a conversation, somehow, and reaches forwards to close it. Not easily. She pushes her hand forwards, she makes her fingers grab the metal arm to pull it in and lock it shut; but her commands are overridden, stopped.

Now the woman comes and sits at the desk. She types a sentence on the typewriter. Just one sentence but slowly, with only one finger. She is poring to find the right letters, but it also seems here there is resistance, dual resistance: her in pressing – she narrows her eyes before each time, and it in the un-press – because she has to use more force than she should. Sometimes we deny what we know.

It is over this time that the storm makes its entrance – you hear it shouting outside but the air that is fast becoming like cotton wool – thick and abrading her throat as she is breathing – is making the sounds distant even though they are just the other side.

She is thrown backwards in the chair and one of her hands

is told to bring up her dress all the way, uncovering her belly. Her eyes are switched off – open but off – and the machine types a response, slow then faster and ranting. Her body is twitching in time to each stroke, and if you looked down you would see it was throwing its words and bruising them onto her baby's house.

The woman stands, suddenly. Gasping for air and bent more and more double. One hand reaches and fumbles open the window. The other is on, then hauls its whole arm round, her belly.

Blood starts to drip through her underwear and onto the ground.

Then starts to crawl, like a line of ants, up the table leg.

Yes, it does.

The woman doesn't see this, but she can feel what is happening. At first, she moves steadily. Out of the attic, down the stairs. But then the blood that is coming from her makes a sudden surge and becomes thicker, as thick as reins. Maybe even as a cord or a bell pull.

The woman starts to run.

As she can – which is hardly at all – out of the house and along the pathway and out of the gate. Once she is out of the gate there is a tearing in the rope of blood that is being drawn up from her into the house. She continues, slower and slower, away from this place and the rain washes away the evidence.

She gets home where she dies on her doorstep, the baby half come out of her. People think she was going to get help

– leaving her house, not coming back to it.

And the writer?

Well, she left the window open.

Fifty-Three

'What's under this?'

I'm with a woman, and she has asked the question.

Out of habit.

I have tossed her the coins and she has taken them and I have taken my bandanna off. A lot of them say it. It doesn't take too much looking to find it. Especially not when fucking, although I try to keep it on then. But even the true professionals seem to like to play at love like kids in yards play house. They say take your clothes off, no, all your clothes, so I strip. I take it off, they look, and they ask. Keep asking it.

I tell her, then I take my purchase and she lays there, me having been the last of her nine to nine.

Whores are romantics. They say I might have lost a truly great love – that strength of despair mirrors strength of love. This one, she said I might have lost something that was at once the peak and the bottom of the whirlpool. I told her whirlpools don't have peaks, they only go down, and she laughed, and took it as an instruction.

So she asked me (as does everyone; it is the question, once I uncover my face) what it meant and I told her what I know.

But when I get Socratic about it at a bar, if it happens to be to, or around, a woman not of disrepute, they (ordinary women) move away because it is possible that they are the one, and we are about – if there was a frissance – to re-eat our own vomit.

I shift my arm, which is being deadened by her hip.

The last one – the last whore but this one - asked about the lessons I could learn. Could have learnt, like relationships are schoolin' and you're aiming for college. I said fuck that. Fuck that to hell.

And –

I don't know why they ask, all of them – why they think and they care. Why? What? How? Why do you think you did it? What do you think happened? How did you do it?

Who? Who do you think it was?

I am tired of these questions, goddamn questions. I have ridden ten thousand trails with them. That is over now. Now I fuck and I drink.

Distractions for my mind from all of the questions, tapping away in my head. I'm almost used to them. Smacking their keys into me.

I am tempted, at this, to feel the scars in my head, but I don't, because I know what they are. That they are there, and what they are. I know them. They don't change. So instead I train my mind to one point on the horizon: the feeling immediately after I typed. That keeps me going: I woke up. And breathed without the crone on my chest.

If I don't get back to that point, if the sun has burnt me too many times on its journey down, at least I can come close to the belief that what I did was right. I mean believe it.

As for the questions. People think they know that love is all. At the least they believe it, because there are things you have to (believe). But they like to be scared. They like to pretend they've run out of honey, they like to think they almost fell in front of that train, they almost tripped and killed themselves. This is why they ask me – I give them exactly what they want: a dead love story.

This woman I am with is now sleeping – or pretending to sleep. Eyes shut closed hand artificially placed on me, to encourage a second purchase, and her long hair that she slowly unbraided in front of me now doing the second part of its performance: abandon(ed). Her eyes are shut and most would believe it, but I know the difference between resting and held closed. So she is 'sleeping', and this makes me alone with their writing.

(The questioners. Dancing in my head.)

First it was her (Danielle). The first woman.

(The first one after the writer.)

With the first questions.

Who picked the weeds and is my mental bourbon companion.

I am removed from the physical. A picture holds up a corner of itself to me: one eye, hair in the wind, her fingers tucking it behind her ear, twice, but it still escapes out, from under her ear and her hat.

She wore big hats to protect her face – just to keep her head from hurting, and she said, 'You ran away from the pain, so you haven't grown. You're a coppiced hedge – stunted.' Or – what are those trees where you go along, and you chop off the centre, you behead the main trunk, so that you get all of those little twigs?

Pollarding. It might be pollarding.

(This lady breathes, slowly, and one lock of it, her hair, ghost-brown, falls from her shoulder and dances on her right breast. Her hand squeezes slightly, as a reflex, and I feel it, my member still within her grip. I do nothing, but I do not move away either. I feel it. It doesn't stop me, though. Questions.)

Have I pollarded myself? Taken away my trunk? One works (the lower trunk), but the other, the aortal one –

It's times like this that I think about going back and asking it to take my eyes. My eyes and my ears. (The things that tempt me.)

She has 'woken', because I responded despite my distraction, to her hand, and now she is waking me fully – the lower me. She is talking to me, though – only half on her job, not even focussed enough to check that I acquiesce in my second coming (ha) and will pay. She is more concerned with the questions – her body is doing its work, her mind is elsewhere. Hypothesising.

She is saying things.

I am not listening. I am thinking this as she is talking – all of this. I don't listen to whores anymore.

I do her once more.

We sleep, I wake.

The light rises.

I am staring at her thigh, well, resting my eyes on it. (I'll keep them, then.) A light dusting of pale hair — soft it had been — and some freckles that a partner should keep track of.

But a blade of light wakes her, diving through a hole in the room's curtain, and she wakes and she straight away returns to her previous talking: she says, again, about the whirlpool, and that puts a bit in my mind and pulls it round to listen. Or at least away from her thigh.

Are highs the chained-to-partners of lows? Are they reflections?

And then it takes itself away again (my mind) — gets the bit between its teeth. And freed now from both my and her leadings, it returns to its obsession

— Danielle/writer/Danielle/writing/written —

and yet with new blood, coming from its mouth: caused by that bit that this whore has dragged through me: it's too late. I have known I could repeat it since her (Danielle), but always thought I was right to leave it, that it should be feared. I thought the relief of losing it showed me its colour (black), but what if what I asked erased was closer to a photograph — shades of sepia but real not the artist's version of it? What if that thing I ran from was not how I have written it?

Was there also good?

And I, also, could have stunted myself — forever dwarfed,

like the plants in the north-most places. Lessons learnt hewn from me.

There are many possibilities, and she's forced me back to them wrenched my head round bloodied my mouth.

In straighter words, she's got me thinking again, this new woman. She spiked that wound and my mind has made some connections. This whore.

...

I think that Danielle, who was first, had meant that pain is valuable, in a bigger circles kind of way, or a seeing the tails of the coin as well as the heads side. (Un-pollarded.)

It was with her I first started thinking that because I hadn't learned the lesson, I could do it again. That was the message I heard. So, she's the one who did it. She planted a bramble in my brain. The original sin.

...

The whore and I dress, and I give her my money.

One

I had left the attic's window open, and it had attracted a dragonfly even though the closest pond is over in the McKinley place – the southest end of Manderley.

I watched as it looped around and around the writer. It wasn't flying lazy circles; it was being forced gradually inwards, closer. Finally it succumbed and whoomph it went down and was sliced by the arms of the keys. Its green was quickly sucked up and the writer was clean again except for the desiccated husk of a dragonfly, which I blew gently onto the floor.

This dragonfly may have been the last of the summer season.

I stared at the letters. What would my first twelve be?

I want her gone

I'd have to move two fingers twice (two ens, two ees), and one finger three times – the space bar – pulling them free, and those four words – which would mean I had started – would then commit me to three more, another eight letters, and twelve finger movements, because I'd planned my wish: from my mind

And then the full stop.

It would have been easier if I could have covered the whole keyboard with my hands, and my fingers could stay and just push down, not tear off each time. But that isn't so – involves contortions beyond hags.

Now a bluebottle was buzzing, mothing in to the typewriter's flame. I looked at the keys and planned my fingers – which would go where, reminding myself which would need to be repeated, and which would need to move for the second set, and so steeling myself for that. After that it was a question of comfort, as my hands wouldn't be moving for a while, so I didn't want to overstretch them.

Swipe – the bluebottle was punched by the reverse swing

of this typewriter – the arms that could go backwards as well as forwards: double jointed. The bluebottle was pushed onto a b, and its life was extracted. Again, I carefully blew off the desiccated husk.

I could close the window, but maybe allowing it the occasional snack would be better. The door was locked. Rafe had the key (my friend). He was a long way away.

I had eaten well. I had rested as well as I could.

I put down the first finger and the key sent its barbed spike up and into me, and then pulled my finger down (somehow) so it pressed into its key, in order to push more blood from me. It didn't shock me because my mind was cold, still, turgid; a lake that was choked thick with weeds.

I remember this, the actions of that day, because it wanted me to, I assume now. It left me her ghost. Left me that. That last shadow of her. It might have been a gift, but more likely it wanted me suspended. Wanted me thirsty and asking is this water poison?

But yes. I typed, and it bit.

I laid the rest of the first sequence, wrenching two fingers up for that n and e which needed doing twice, pulling the keys with me. Then I tore three fingers free – taking a chocolate chip chunk out of each – and reassigned two.

I pressed, and repressed, keys:

from my mind

And the full stop.

.

My head was whisked downwards onto the uplifted keys which spelled I want her gone from my mind, and it was done.

Rafe woke me, stood waiting with a cold cider. He'd already tipped me away from the machine so I was slumped back against the chair.

'The question is, why did you want her gone enough to go through all this?' He handed me the drink and I looked up at him through what felt like ant-allergy eyes. Rafe added, 'It's done a good job – I'm your best friend and I don't know who she is. Was.' He added, 'I doubt she does either. If she still exists.'

There were words on the paper, highlighted by my drippings, held behind the paper-guide. Her/gone/mind.

He handed me a mirror and in it, across my forehead was a mash of jumbled keys. It had danced a jig on my forehead. Swollen forehead that would never lose its work of Shakespeare in Remington-style letters. But a clear story, running through the mass of letters: words for me.

I must have been in love.

THE RED KING

NICHOLAS BRODIE

The Red King: Francis Holloway, late 20s, fled Australia after orchestrating a terrible event, and arrived in the United States of America. He immediately went on the run, eluding authorities for months, until he realised he could not run any longer and managed to find solace in the small icy town of Whittier, Alaska, under a false identity. Six years later, he is about to realise that his time of judgment has arrived.

One

Six months before war was declared, two policemen were preparing to kick down the door of a man's apartment in Whittier, Alaska on suspicion of murder. It was descending into winter, so the sun wasn't to rise for another ninety minutes. The men proceeded down the cold hallway of Begich Tower in a slow, predatory manner, torches held alongside their gun to help guide them, both of them fearful of waking anyone that wasn't the perpetrator and bringing more unwanted attention their way.

The police of Whittier were right to feel unappreciated, maybe even unwanted: twelve months ago they were relocated from the second floor of the forty-two floor tower, to the basement, outvoted three-to-one in favour of the grocer who wanted to expand his space and use the station as a clothing shop and compete with the sole other clothing shop, Clothes 'R' Us, which was on the sixteenth floor and had serviced the entire building, thus almost all of Whittier, alone, for thirty-four years. When the public had the opportunity to vote between continuing an almost invisible police presence, versus a wider selection in jeans and shirts and sneakers that didn't include just blue and black and white, the result was unanimous.

They'd also borne the brunt of a public call to reduce their wages, which had been reduced by fifteen per cent only eighteen months earlier already, resulting in two police officers quitting—or demanding relocation, if you were in the know—shortly after. The argument was this: there simply wasn't enough crime to justify a continued police presence at Begich Tower, 1 Norwich Road, Whittier. The fulltime staff were now two: Sergeant Donovan, and an officer, Matthew Corrigan, with one additional officer, James Wallace, employed on a casual basis, splitting his time between Whittier and Anchorage, about ninety minutes away. It was these two officers who were now stepping lightly down the hallway on the sixteenth floor, each stretching their baton away from their body, in order to guarantee maximum silence.

The Sergeant, Arthur Donovan, had issued the order for the arrest an hour earlier. He was now in the shower, scrubbing at such a slow pace he occasionally forgot if he had washed certain parts of his body or not. It wasn't due to his advanced age—he simply had a lot on his mind. In two hours, a town meeting would be called and he had to look his best. Not a single hair could be out of place. He would announce that long-time Whittier resident Francis Holloway had been arrested for the murder of newcomer Tarek Nasser, a husband to Reem Nasser and father of three young girls, Rokan, Perla and Yara, all under the age of twelve. This would guarantee the station's existence for another decade at least, he figured, scrubbing at his armpit, maybe even a pay rise and another full-time officer. Maybe, he thought, holding back a smile, we could go back on to the second floor. Kick out the grocer and take over the old space and incorporate the grocery as a holding cell. Get an all-for-one deal. He knew the likelihood of this happening was next to nil but he couldn't help smirking at the thought of it.

What made this murder so special was that it was the first one committed in Begich Tower, the building that housed ninety per cent of the population of Whittier. As far as people could remember, it was the first murder committed in the town, period.

Later, during questioning, Francis will admit to visiting the bar where the body was found. He will admit to drinking heavily. That was undeniable; any witness could attest to that even if they hadn't been there. He will concede that he spoke with Tarek Nasser for a while and got angry with him, but he will not admit to why that was the case. That was for him and him alone to understand. But he will say he did not kill him, and he will be adamant about it. But this is still all a few hours away from happening. Right now, he is fast asleep, under a thick white quilt, an office trashcan doubling as a puke bucket by the side of the bed.

'Do you know him?' James whispered as he tiptoed down the hallway. He'd agreed to work Fridays and Saturdays in Whittier every week. It was a few extra hundred in the bank for less work than he'd ever perform in Anchorage. He had a new-born baby daughter to take care of, and besides, he didn't mind the commute from Anchorage. It was the only time he could listen to music the way he preferred: loud, as if the speakers were about to explode. Two months into the job and he was still surprised at how well people knew each other here. On his third shift he mentioned to one of the tenants, in passing, that he was a huge Neil Diamond fan and the following week he was handed an old vinyl of Beautiful Noise by another.

'Frank? Yeah. He's all right. Never spoke to him much or anything. But all right.' Matt replied, motioning for him to stop so he could listen to a sudden burst of sound. It was an alarm clock. They kept moving. 'I don't understand how he's under arrest already though.'

'What do you mean? The murder happened a few days ago, didn't it? Probably had time to review the video by now.'

'What? No. It happened tonight. Five hours ago.'

What had happened was this. A bored teenage boy, Jake, who lived on a different floor to Francis, was walking along each hallway in the Begich Tower condominium in an attempt to stave off the dullness of insomnia. When he reached the second floor, Jake came across the open door to Jim's Tavern. Usually, in such situations, given his younger age, he would stay away, as the sight of him inside a bar would alert his father—who knows Jimmy personally, as does literally everyone else in the building—resulting in an immediate grounding and complete loss of television and visiting-mates privileges. But, given he was in the middle of his high school exams, he didn't see the difference, and being that it was three in the morning on a Monday and most of the building was fast asleep, he was feeling slightly more daring than usual, and so he stepped inside, ready to run out at the sight of anyone at all and race back to his home on the thirty-second floor, where his father, a deep sleeper, would be none the wiser. This was how he came across the victim, Tarek Nasser, slumped over the bar. His head was resting in what Jake later learned was a pool of blood. He thought he was just asleep, until he got close and saw that his face had been caved in.

That was one part of what the police knew. The boy had screamed and run home to tell his father, Richard. He desperately shook him awake and in a state of annoyance his Dad put his dressing gown on and went down to the tavern to see exactly what on earth his son had confused for a dead man. In an effort to get the victim's attention—shaking him by the shoulder—Tarek toppled off the bar stool and collapsed onto the floor with a heavy bump, causing his face to now face upwards, showing the full extent of the damage. Unsure as to what to do next, and ignoring the panicked screams of his son, he tried lifting the man back onto the stool, at which point Jake managed to coherently suggest that doing so might disturb the crime scene more than it already had been. And so Richard carefully placed the man back onto the floor and they both raced down the stairs to the police station to explain everything and account for the blood of another man on their dressing gown and pyjamas, along with any fingerprints or whatever else the cops would be able to find.

Matt had been the one to interview Richard, taking his bloodied fingerprints and swabbing under his nails for evidence that either would or would not back up the story of innocence he was eagerly pushing. 'You gotta believe me, Matt,' Richard had said, eyes pleading, Jake sitting next to him and staring at the floor. 'Our kids play football together.'

Jake had been equally forthcoming. 'I didn't do it Mr. Corrigan, I swear. I swear on me mum's life. I just saw the guy lying there, like he was drunk or something, and then I saw all the blood, I mean, I think it was blood—it looked like blood even though the lights were all off—and I freaked out, man, I mean Mr. Corrigan. I just fucking ran straight back home, sorry, I mean I just ran home and got Dad and he… he didn't mean to touch him. It was dark in there. You, you gotta believe us. I swear this is what happened.'

Matt sighed. He didn't know what to do. He felt bad about listing Jake or Richard as suspects, for a murder of all things. All things considered, the two of them were good members of the community. Jake worked casually as a cashier at the grocery and yes, he could be annoying, like the few occasions when he'd short-changed him and had insisted otherwise, or the general insufferable attitude all young men displayed at this age in life, so close to adulthood but seemingly still a long way away, but apart from that he was a good kid. And Richard. Richard had helped with his mother's finances for the past twenty years with barely a complaint, which had always impressed Matt, given his mother's dislike of keeping receipts and accepting help of any kind. But, still, a murder? Here? He'd dealt with multiple homicides when he'd been stationed in Seattle, years ago, which is why he'd taken the opportunity to move to Whittier, despite everyone's insistence otherwise. He didn't see it as a trap, a career-killer. It was an opportunity to be one with the community, he'd told his fiancé—now wife—at the time, without the threat of being killed on the job, what with all the protests occurring back home. No one did anything here except shoplift once in a while—how bad could it get? He was starting to like the friendly greetings, the way no one told him to fuck off. What would happen now? Was the next step in this thing a riot? How could one riot in a building this tall? It was too cold to do it outside. People here spent whole winters indoors, never once leaving the building. So what now? This murder was starting to annoy him.

He did the only thing he could do, given the circumstances. He called the Sergeant. It was the last thing he wanted to do, given the Sergeant's short temper, but what else was there?

Donavan answered on the sixth ring.

'Why the fuck are you ringing me at two in the morning?' It was a fair question. The overnight shift was purely to justify their existence. Everyone knew nothing happened, but that was beside the point. If you remove the overnight shift, then you begin to justify the argument that an already reduced police presence could therefore be reduced even further. The vote was already in favour of reducing the overnight shift to Thursday, Friday and Saturday only, and it was usually given to the casual, James, but he'd had this night rostered off for weeks as his son was in an after-hours school play. And so Matt had drawn the short straw, which, given his lower ranking, he always would.

With a yawn Matt elaborated on what had just been explained to him moments earlier. He peered through the plastic slits over the window of the Sergeant's office, watching Jake and Richard wait for his return, studying their polarising reactions to this whole thing: on the one hand there was Jake, occupied by his phone, probably texting his friends about what had happened, his face completely consumed by the bright glow of the device, his expressions occurring as if what had just happened had existed in a whole other universe away from this one; then there was his father, arms crossed firmly over his chest, a vacant stare the only sign he was still awake, the event consuming him whole.

'Okay. Interview Jake; see if you can get any further information from him. Do it in private, I don't want his Dad interrupting with his usual bullshit that will get me in trouble six months down the track, if this ever reaches court. After you interview him, ring me back. Got it?'

And so Matt ordered Jake into the Sergeant's office. It was the only suitable interview room, given Richard insisted on waiting around, and the holding cell simply wouldn't do. Matt placed his work phone on the table, the standard police recording devices having been sent to Anchorage last January due to their years of non-use. He opened the recording app and pressed the digitised red button and asked Jake to describe, in minutia detail, what had happened, and so Jake repeated what he'd told Matt earlier, getting increasingly annoyed at Matt's constant interruptions, with questions such as How many steps did you take between the front door and the body? and How did you know it was blood if the lights were off?

'You just know. What else is going to come out of some guy's head?'

Matt scratched his chin. 'Tell me again what you did once you saw the victim.'

Jake threw his arms out in frustration. 'Why are we still here? Shouldn't you be down there, checking it out or whatever?'

'An officer is currently viewing the site.' Both of them knew that wasn't true, but he needed to get the story straight for the Sergeant before anything else could happen. It's just how it had always been. 'What happened after you saw the victim?'

'I ran! What do you think? I fucking ran! I got the hell out of there.'

Matt sighed. 'Okay, but more specifically, did you run the whole time, all the way back home? Or did you just run out the door and walk the rest of the way to the elevator? What did you do?'

'Shit, I don't know. Maybe I ran maybe I stopped halfway. Did a fucking, I don't know, handstand or whatever. Does it really matter?'

Matt felt bad for pressing Jake so hard, considering he was about to enter his final exam period, but he needed to extract something, anything, that he could pass on to the Sergeant. Without it, he'd have to keep them here and Jake needed sleep if he was going to start preparing for it. There were posters along each hallway with the entire exam schedule, so everyone knew when to keep quiet. The maths test was in thirty-three hours, on floor six. 'Yes, Jake, yes it does. If you want to clear your name—you're not a suspect, I want to be clear, but that might change later if things don't add up—so I need you to answer my questions to keep you ruled out for later.'

'Fine.' He scratched his nose and stared at the ceiling, desperately searching for all fragments of memory among the haze of the past few hours. 'I guess I freaked out when I saw the body there and I, like, ran out of the bar then, but then I kind of walked to the elevator in a bit of a daze after like a hundred feet. It freaked me out, man.'

'Of course. I understand.' Matt had seen a few dead bodies during his time in Seattle, and New York before that as a rookie. He'd been stationed at Whittier for eight years now and, while he'd forgotten most of the people he'd arrested, he could still remember that body he was called in for during his first month on the force: frozen, sitting on a bench, as if waiting for someone who never arrived. 'So, from the elevator you did what?'

'I hit the button for my floor and then when the lift got up and the doors opened, I ran back inside and woke up Dad and told him what happened. I was shitting myself. He's... you know what he's like about staying up late, especially with these exams coming up.'

'Sure.' He didn't know if he'd got what the Sergeant needed, and he didn't want to call him back prematurely, so he asked another question to ensure he'd be happy with the result of the interview, even though he knew what the response would be. He'd only ever interviewed six other people in Whittier before, all for minor indiscretions, three of which were related to the same crime: vandalising. He'd hit that number on his first day in New York.

He was starting to feel like a rookie again. 'When you were walking to the elevator after seeing the body, did you see anyone?'

'I don't think so. It was all a daze, like I said.'

'What about after you got off the elevator to go home?'

'Um, no, no one.'

Matt leaned back in his chair and coughed, a weak attempt to suffocate the futility of this conversation. It all felt pointless, a waste of everyone's time. This murder was not going to go away anytime soon.

Then Jake leaned forward. 'Wait, actually. Yeah, I did see someone.'

Matt went still. 'Who? Can you name them?'

'I didn't see his face. It was some guy walking down the hallway, away from me. He disappeared into the stairwell on level two, the one at the other end, long before I got onto the elevator.'

Matt scribbled down notes. 'Can you identify anything about this person? The colour of the clothes they were wearing? Was he black, was he white, was he Asian? What kind of haircut? Anything.'

'It was a short cut, like he'd had a buzz cut a few weeks ago and it was growing out again. He had a black jacket on, and blue jeans. Maybe early thirties? He was just walking along, I never saw his face.'

'Anything else? Was he tall, short? What kind of shoes? Was there anything significant about the way he was walking?'

Jake scrunched his nose. 'He had a slight limp, I think? I don't know; it was all a rush. Everything was dark. Why?'

Matt smiled. There it was. 'Thanks for your time, Jake. You can wait out there with your Dad. We'll let you know if we need anything further.'

'Can we get water or coffee or something?'

Matt pointed to where the kitchen was and directed him out of the office. He watched the two of them huddle around the boiling kettle, mumbling to one another, and he called the Sergeant to let him know that Jake had identified a man with short hair who walks with a limp wandering level two at the same time of the murder. They only knew of one person in the building who fit this description. The Sergeant called it in and rang James to tell him he was rostered on after all then went into his own kitchen and made a coffee, ready for the arrival of Francis Holloway.

When the policemen woke Francis, softly knocking on the door, then heavily, once it became clear it would be the only way for him to hear them, he stared at them blankly as they apologised for waking him, his short hair poking out at odd angles, and apologised again when they explained they needed to cuff him and bring him to the station for questioning about a murder that had occurred only a few hours prior. He rubbed his eyes, the hangover well and truly in effect, and asked if he could shower first—he couldn't—so he asked if he could change out of his t-shirt and boxers and make a coffee then—yes, absolutely, and could you make us both one too, the officers nodded, walking inside.

As he stirred the sugar through the three coffees, all without milk, he thought back to the scene in Melbourne, years ago, when he was running away from that explosion, hailing a taxi to take him to the airport. The explosion he had created and devised and planned through with thorough execution with a team of six others. The one that had caused an international manhunt yet was still unsolved.

He wondered why they weren't arresting him for that.

NO SECOND CHANCES

CAREY DENTON

So here we are, Charlie and I, settling things the only way we know how.

Low lying clouds hug the top of the peaks, and the chairlift slides us up into their damp embrace. I raise the safety bar and as we slip off, the wind whips across and catches up a scraping of snow flinging it like darts.

Charlie skis with the balletic grace of an instructor. She glides by, looping the straps of her poles onto her wrists and adjusting her goggles. I gyrate my shoulders and crack my knees, remembering the London rush-hour-traffic and the long drive down from Calais yesterday.

We both know Charlie's the better skier. She's super fit, and she's skied this run a thousand times more than me. Her eyes are hidden behind her reflective goggles, but the twist of her mouth tells me she thinks she's got the race in the bag. That's the thing about Charlie; she doesn't really understand what makes a winner. I haven't been at the stock exchange for thirteen years without learning something about gaining an edge. This run was always the decider between us. If we were boys, I suppose it might have been a penalty shoot-out or a pissing contest. As it is, we race.

I've kept the chalet going over the years, and I've spent a shedload of my money on it, while Charlie's drifted from one thing to the next. Why should she get to decide what happens to it now?

Charlie is looking down the slope. She doesn't wear a helmet, and she looks in the zone. I'm buzzing, psyching myself up. I don't need to beat her down the ridge, in fact I want her out in front.

'Count us in,' she says.

Smug devil's giving me the advantage.

My breath is short and steamy. I count fast and pole off hard. I don't even look to see if she's coming. No second chances.

I hug the outer edge of the ridge and stay low with my knees bent and poles hooked into my armpits. The piste is rutted with ice; it's like skiing over corrugated sheeting. The vibrations rattle my teeth. Ten seconds in and I feel the burn pulsing up my legs. I'm waiting for Charlie to pass. She doesn't. Where is she? Perhaps she didn't get off? Tough. I'm not stopping. I stick to my plan. I turn sharp to the right, and Charlie is there. My stomach loops out and settles with a bang at the back of my neck, and I forget the pain in my legs. Are we going to collide, or is she going to get past?

How fast are we going? Sixty miles an hour? Eighty?

Too fast to take in details, and yet I do. Charlie doesn't look around but a slight twitch of her head tells me she knows I'm there. Her hair is flying straight up and her jacket is ballooned with air. She starts to come out of her crouch, perhaps she's thinking she can turn with me, in front of me, out of my way – but it's too late for that. If I edge my skis, just a fraction, it might give her time to run past, but it will slow me down. I might miss the bend. If I hit the bank I'll crash and then she'll win for sure. I stay on course.

She's past, and then I feel it. My ski touches hers. I wobble. The ice is smooth blue under my skis – like a skate rink. I let my body go fluid, try not to overcompensate. I don't hear or see what happens to Charlie, but there is a movement in the air, a shift in my slipstream that doesn't feel right. I take the next bend and come upright and try to edge. The ice is making everything too fast. I want to win, but I don't want to die. To my left I see a dark shape flying in the bowl.

We call it the bowl: you can ski all the sides down to the funnel that re-joins the run, but they're damn steep and carved into massive great moguls. In the morning, in the shade, it's like skiing ice boulders. What's flapping in there? A bird circling low? I should be focussed on the run, taking advantage of my lead, but something makes me ease up so that I can glance over. It's not circling: it's falling.

Charlie is on the ground with her skis below her and I imagine that at any second she will catch an edge and right herself. Then she tips off the top of a mogul and becomes airborne. She flails slightly in the air, like a jumper readying to land, but as she hits the ground she loses a ski. It ricochets away, tip over tail. She slides at speed and takes off again. It must be sheet ice down there. She sails through the air, misses two moguls and when she lands she throws her sticks uphill, looking for purchase. A pole rips out of her hands, taking a glove with it, and her other ski twists off her foot.

When did I stop skiing? I am poised on the rim of the basin panting hot white breath and watching my sister plunge down the slope. I have a strange feeling that I should be able to put a stop to this, as if I'm watching some action movie that has got all too much, and a click of the remote can bring calm to the screen.

Each time Charlie hits the ground, she loses another bit of equipment. The last pole, another glove, her goggles and then a boot. Surely, that's not even possible.

Her body slows as she reaches the shallow bottom of the bowl. I drag off a glove and fumble for my phone, keying in the emergency number with thick, clumsy fingers. I don't recognise the controlled voice that asks for help.

I tip over the edge. Every muscle in my body is wound tight: I must relax or it'll be me bouncing down the boulders. Charlie is a dark stain in the shadows. Unmoving. Perhaps she's unconscious? I reach the bottom and she still hasn't moved. I step out of my skis and drop to my knees; there's no give in my boots and it's like falling onto concrete. I reach out a gloved hand, and as I touch her she groans and begins to unfold.

'Careful,' I say. 'Wait for the wagon.'

She mumbles into her jacket. I pat her shoulder gently and there is a ripple of movement under my hand. Did she just shrug me off?

Her face is a mess: eyelids as squishy as over-ripe fruit, and a smear of blood at each nostril. Her cheekbones have disappeared beneath a puff of flesh, and through cracked lips I can see a dark space where a tooth should be.

She's trying to talk, and I lean low, tilting my head around so that I feel and hear the hiss of air through the new, toothless, gap.

'You cut me up you cow!'

At the chalet, Greg presses a hipflask of brandy into my hand before he drives us down the mountain to the hospital.

He asks me how it happened, and when I don't answer he doesn't ask again. I sip at the brandy and a hot burn replaces the acid anxiety in my gut.

Greg sighs. 'What's so important about the chalet anyway?' he says.

The rush of the river, churning over boulders and matching the bends in the road turn for turn, masks the silence. I can hardly tell him it represents that moment in my life when the future still held endless possibilities.

'She'll be all right,' he says, and squeezes my knee.

When we turn into the car park, Charlie is sitting on a low wall smoking. She has no shoes, so her socked feet dangle like a child's. She stubs out the cigarette in the scrubby flowerbed behind her, and eases herself off the wall one buttock at a time. She takes the four steps to the car in eight, holding herself very still and upright. I get out and help her into the passenger seat.

'You owe me a tooth,' she says.

I do not feel bad. I am not going to feel bad. And what's more, I won the fucking race.

When we get back Charlie goes to bed. Greg is on the phone to the children, but I wave the mobile away when he holds it out to me. Afterwards we sit down to cold meats, a Camembert, and bread. I'm thinking I won't eat, but then I fall on the food like I'm starved.

'You know,' I say, 'I always thought I might have a season out here.'

'Like Charlie,' Greg says.

I snort. 'Yeah. Only she had ten.'

He raises his eyebrows.

'Well seven at least,' I say.

I follow him into the kitchen and stand with my back against the counter, looking out over the valley. The town has tripled in size since Mum and Dad bought the place when we were kids. The conseil will pay top price to build the new lift on this site – we'll never get that sort of money again.

Greg is wiping down the work surfaces. He doesn't look at me.

'It's not too late,' he says, although he knows as well as me there's never enough time or money, and sometimes I can't remember what came first, the salary or the lifestyle.

Late in the day I decide to ski again. As I'm leaving I bump into Charlie coming downstairs. She walks delicately, as if testing each step against the pain running up her body.

'We still have to decide about the chalet,' she says.

'It's your call,' I say, and even I am surprised to hear the news. 'I'm sorry I cut you up. All right?'

Charlie is poised on the bottom step of the stairs, still absorbing the fact that she's got her way over the chalet. She looks blank then barks out a laugh, which makes her hug her sore ribs.

'Shit, I knew you were going to turn high. That's why I hung back. Thought you'd bottle it. Always knew you were stubborn, but I didn't think you'd die for the place.'

'It wasn't me that nearly died, Charlie,' I say.

'Oh, yeah.' She grins her new, gappy grin. 'Want to change your mind about letting me sell the house now?'

I have so much I could say, but instead I walk out.

It's turned into a perfect blue-sky day, and I go back to the ridge we were on this morning. From the top of the lift I veer off the piste and start to climb, my skis first sinking through powder, then gliding when they hit the hard-pack a foot down. I round the side of the mountain and I'm looking out over a vista of peaks that march all the way to the border.

The sun is low, and the light is clear and sharp as it bounces back off the snow. Nothing moves, even the sky is cloud-free. I collapse down, and snow drifts up around me like a duvet. I take my helmet off and lift my face, eyes closed, to the last heat of the day.

Behind my eyelids I see Charlie's flying body: black on white. How come she just walked away? She really is a jammy sod.

We still have the drive home, and I tense at the prospect of the hours of autoroute ahead, and Monday morning back at my desk doing a job I've lost my love for. I open my eyes to the peaks.

I try to picture a conversation with Greg where I suggest we walk away from our London life, take the kids out of their private schools and sack the nanny. And then I understand that this is the most frightening thing of all. If no one is asking anything of me, what will I choose?

Below, there's a sweep of virgin powder. It doesn't look impossible, although it's hard to know what lies over that drop. The sun's going down fast, and it pinks the horizon as it wedges between two distant peaks. I'm wired with possibility as I push off and feel the snow's soft give as it splits around my calves and dusts my face with its icy spray.

IDEAS I AM SENDING ON HOLIDAY

CLAUDIE WHITTAKER

Fox House: From the outside, Fox House is a gracious, well-proportioned Georgian manor, with lavender-edged paths punctuated every six feet by perfectly pruned box balls. Presiding over the spacious consulting room, behind the biggest, most antique desk in the county, sits Dr Bernard Thompson. This eminent consultant psychiatrist, already on a pedestal by dint of his profession, is hoisted ever higher by his blameless patients, his obligated employees and his diamond-studded wife. Bernard does exactly what he wants, and gets away with it, because he is cleverer and more devious than everyone else. Only his dogs, and possibly his wife, know the truth, but they will never talk. When runaway Jo arrives to manage his practice, she soon uncovers a world of chaos and corruption behind the façade. Just how many of his patients has Bernard bedded? To what lengths will he go to cover it up? The closer Jo gets to the terrifying truth, the more relentlessly is she drawn into conflict with a cold-blooded murderer whose latest victim lies in a coma. Can Jo stop him from finishing the job? Can she save herself?

The following extract began life as an exercise in character development written as an inner monologue. Young Alastair rescues himself from the wine cellar in which he was locked by his abusive, psychopathic mother.

She's blinking, looking round. She hasn't seen me. The cellar's too dark. She can't see past the rectangle of light. The bottle's outside the light. She walks forward. Her foot goes on the bottle. The bottle slides. She loses her balance. She looks funny. Her arms are all wobbly and her legs go up in the air. My secret tummy laughs. She falls down, crack, like a big egg breaking. The bottle spins like it will never stop. There's blood on her head. I see it pour out and mix with the wine. She's peeping at me. She doesn't move. I keep still as a statue. Then she reaches for the shelves but falls back. She peeps at me again. The bottle is slowing down at last. I don't like the scraping noise it makes on the flagstones. I don't like the way she's quiet. Peeping at me. I hate it. I run out and shut the door, turning the key. I press my ear to the door. She's whispering. Her voice sounds like her mouth is full of socks.

'Alastair, let me out. You're being very naughty. This is a very naughty thing to do. If you don't let me out right now I'll call the police and you'll be taken away. Alastair.'

I put the bottle by the cellar door, on the floor on its side. She'll come down soon. She must have heard the breaking glass. I made a LOT of noise on purpose. There's a horrible smell. I don't like it. It's dark, the smell. I enjoyed smashing those bottles. The floor's slippery. I creep to the door, stand against the wall beside it. I wonder if she'll trip over the bottle. I hope so.

She must have come downstairs like a quiet little mouse. Normally, she's noisy like a dragon. Cunning, like a fox. She can always tell if I've been naughty. She can tell more than I can. She's got a Lair. Upstairs. A fox's home is a den. I know that. She thinks I don't, which makes me cunning like a fox too. She likes locking me in her Lair, in the dark, but I've never been locked in the cellar before. I've been really naughty, again, but I don't know what I've done. I never know. She says I'm bad.

'No Mummy, I don't want to!' I used to cry. 'Let me out, please! Mummy!'

'I'll let you out when you've learnt your lesson, Alastair. YOU KNOW WHAT YOU DID.'

'I don't know what I did Mummy. What did I do?' I would say this EVERY TIME, when I was six. Now I'm seven. One day I said, 'I'm sorry, Mummy, I didn't mean to.'

'Really! That's a first! You promise to never do it again, and I'll let you out. Never let the wickedness take over. If you do, I'll lock you up again. UNDERSTAND?'

'Yes, Mummy.' She had let me out quicker than normal but she hurt my arm.

This time, I haven't cried, or said sorry. I'm waiting. At first, I didn't know what to do because it's worse than the Lair. Webby and very, very cold. I'm seven and grown up. I don't want to stay down here anymore.

'Alastair? What have you done?' She's really loud and angry. Right outside the door. The key grates in the lock. The wall is cold behind my back. I don't want her to see me.

The door opens. It doesn't creak. I see a rectangle of light on the floor and her shadow in the middle of it. I look at her shadow face, then at her real face. It's all red apart from the skin round her mouth which is white. This means she's really, really angry.

The last time I saw those colours on her face was when Daddy died. I wasn't in the room. She was. She said it was my fault and I must never talk about it or I would be put in a prison full of scary men who would hurt me. I didn't understand why it was my fault, but I believed her because she's clever. I'm the cleverest boy in my class, but she's much cleverer than me. She always knows what I'm thinking. She can make me think in different ways to how I want.

She's stopped whispering. Silly Mummy. No phone in the cellar. I know that. I listen a bit more. I walk upstairs, smiling a lot. I can't stop. I'm starving because I've been shut in the cellar all day with nothing to eat. I'm going to make a sandwich. I know how to do that. Easy-peasy. First I take my clothes off. I hate that smelly old wine. I stand on a chair and get everything out. I make peanut butter, marmite and cheese sandwiches. I put the bread together. I put jam on top. I smile and smile at the thought that she can't do anything. I won't think about what will happen when I let her out. I might never.

Should I call 999 like when Daddy died? I know about 999. I know my address. Only silly people don't know their addresses. If I call 999 people will come and let her out. They'll be cross. After they leave, she'll be a dragon and she'll lock me in her Lair. She always does when anyone comes and she's had to be nice to me in front of them.

If she was dead she couldn't be a dragon. If I leave her there she'll probably die. I know about death. I know about bleeding. I'm a very clever boy. Only she's cleverer, except this time. I want her to leave me alone for ever. If she wasn't here, I would never be locked in the Lair again. Is she frightened? I can't imagine her being frightened like me.

Will people blame me? She said Daddy died because of me, but I know that isn't true because I wasn't in the same room. She was in there shouting. There was a LOT of noise. But I didn't know what happened because I was very young then. I was five. Now I'm seven and I know a lot. If she had killed Daddy, she should have gone to prison. I know that. But no-one thought she had killed him. She said he had fallen off his stepladder. I didn't think that was true because Daddy hated climbing things and never did. When I crept in to see Daddy she put them on the floor, the stepladders. The ambulance took him away. He didn't move. She said I wasn't to say that I saw her bring them in from the garage when he was already on the floor. She said if I told she would make sure I was locked away for ever, with the baddest people in the world. Seven is quite grown up, which she doesn't realise. I have read a LOT. She doesn't know. Even my teacher doesn't know how well I can read. If I tell her she might send me away or say it's a trick and I'm lying. She might shut me in the classroom cupboard. My teacher has long, brown hair. It's shiny. I'm not scared of her like I'm scared of HER but I don't believe her a lot of the time. I would never say that out loud. My thoughts are my thoughts. Now that I'm seven, I can easily keep my thoughts in my head. I know what happens if I let them out. Danger.

If I call 999 now they will see my smelly clothes. They might ask questions I don't want to answer. Like what was I doing in the cellar. I can't tell them because she would be cross. But if she's dead, she can't be cross. I stop eating my sandwich and put my fingertips together, like baddies do, 'cos I feel like a baddy too, sort of.

I go upstairs and put on clean clothes, drop the dirty ones in the basket. I've been able to dress myself since I was three. Some children at school need help to change for PE. They must be pathetic. She called me pathetic when I said I wanted to be called Bernard. Why would I want to be named after a pathetic wimp? She meant Daddy. She called me Alastair, my grandfather's name, who's dead too. I hate it. Bernard's a clever name. If I was a Bernard I'd be like Daddy, but alive.

Has she died by now? I creep down the steps and listen hard. She's being quiet as a mouse again. Is it a trick? She would play a trick like that. If I open the door now, she might peep at me. I hated that.

I whisper, 'Mummy.' Again, louder. I think about all the blood, and her falling back when she tried to reach the shelf. I think she died after she stopped whispering. But she could be doing what I did. Pretending. I think of my sandwich. I creep back upstairs and sit at the table. I can't stop smiling. No Mummy to tell me what to do. No Mummy to confuse me. No Mummy to hurt me. No Mummy to shout at me. No Mummy to lock me up. No Mummy to make me hungry. No Mummy.

I make another sandwich. I can have as many as I want: ten if I want. I pour a glass of milk. I take my plate and glass to the big sofa, where she always sits. I put them on the little table and pick up the remote. She watches telly at night. I'm allowed to watch David Attenborough sometimes. She says I can't watch children's programmes because they're bad for the brain. But once she switched one on when I was there. I wanted to watch it, at first. Before it had finished, she dragged me into the Lair. She said I had been very naughty for watching it. When I said it was her idea, she called me a liar. I stayed in the Lair all night. I wet myself. I couldn't help it.

Don't think about it! I push the idea out. It's going on holiday, that idea. A lot of my ideas do that when I want them to. I can make them leave and never come back but sometimes they burst out, which makes me sad, but I never let her see. Or they make me angry, fizzing like fireworks in my tummy. She can't hear them.

I watch a children's programme about a dog. It's stupid. The people who made the story must be stupid. Maybe she's right. It's disappointing.

I creep down the steps again to listen. Nothing. What can I do to make sure? Open the door? Will I be able to see her properly? How can I see her properly? I know: the torch in the kitchen which I'm not allowed to touch. I know how it works. I took it out once when she was in the shower. When she came down, she asked what I'd been up to. I said, 'Doing my reading'. She didn't say anything. I was very pleased because I'd lied and she'd believed it, instead of the other way round when I told the truth and she told me I was lying.

If I unlock the door quickly and shine the torch in I'll be able to see her. If she moves I'll lock the door quickly. If she's dead she won't move. I'll be able to tell because I know about blood and dying. I want to wait a bit longer. It's after tea time. It'll be dark soon and I'm very tired. I'll go to bed for a bit and when I wake up I'll come back down and see. I go to my bedroom. Mummy, I'm taking the torch upstairs. You can't do anything.

I lie down. Smiling and smiling. She can't do a thing. It's very funny.

It's morning. I know because I can hear birds singing. Mummy! I jump out of bed, pick up the torch, creep like a fox to the cellar door. Quiet. Nothing. Then I think, I can pull out the key and shine the torch through the keyhole. I might be able to see her.

I pull out the big, heavy key. I drop it on the step. Clunk. Freeze! It's OK, I haven't unlocked the door yet. I wait for her to say something. I look through the keyhole into pitch black. I shine the torch in and try to put my eye beside it but there's not enough room for both and I can't see anything. I've got to open the door. I put the key back in the lock, and it grates when I push it round. I turn the handle, pull the door towards me, and shine the torch in. Her eyes are looking. Not at me. They're looking at nothing but they're open. There's a funny smell. A mixture of smelly wine and blood. I know the smell of dried blood. I shine the torch at her for a bit longer to make sure. There are lots of broken bottles. The one she tripped over is there. She's still, like a dead rock.

I know it's safe to leave the door open. Deep down inside, I can't trust her to stay there if I leave it open, even though I know she's dead, so I lock her in again.

'My Mummy has fallen over in some wine, and she won't wake up,' I say to the person at 999. She said to stay where I was and someone would come.

I run downstairs to unlock the door and open it so they won't guess I locked her in. I put the key in my pocket. Then I run back up and wait in the front garden.

A woman in a uniform jumps out of the ambulance. I

like it. It's big with blue lights. Will I be allowed to go in the ambulance? A police car comes around the corner, its siren really loud. People are looking out of their windows. I remember I can't be excited because Mummy's dead so I make my face sad. I put my thumb in my mouth, for the first time ever. It's nice.

'Hello, young man,' the woman says. She looks kind but I don't think she can be. 'What's your name? Can you take me to your Mummy?'

I pull out my thumb with a plop. 'My name is Bernard. Mummy's in the cellar.'

Then I send all my ideas on holiday. Nearly all. I keep clever, grown-up Bernard. I like him.

ROADS

JOHN DOWN

'Roads' is taken from John's first novel, British Teeth, which is about a man trying to put himself back together as his country falls apart.

John Hay returns to his hometown, Plymouth, for his mother's funeral, a year after the death of his girlfriend, Rebecca, in a road accident, which caused his life to finally unravel. This culminated in a brutal assault, but he cannot remember what provoked it.

He tries to piece together the past and make sense of the overwhelming present using the story of his own life, the stories of others, and stories of his own invention.

British Teeth looks at why we leave, remain and return, at the consequences of our decisions, and how ordinary people live through extraordinary times.

'It all started like this. I'm driving down the High Street, it's a beautiful day, not a cloud in the sky, and this lad's strolling across the road like he owns it. He looks at me coming towards him and the look on his face just made me so angry. When he stepped out in front of me, I knew I could stop but I realised just then, just for that moment, I didn't have to. He looked right at me and I couldn't stop looking in his eyes and as I got closer, I saw them change. He stopped looking at me like he was better than me, like I was trespassing on his land. He was afraid. He was afraid because he knew I weren't stopping. And I thought, just before I hit him, when we was inches apart, you're still perfect now. You're still perfect until I hit you and break you. If you can be so perfect, so beautiful, such a beautiful boy on such a beautiful day, how come you turned into such a c__t? Is it just the world that makes us like this? You know, society and the government and that, or is it just in us? Just in us from the moment we're born, before that even, and we can't escape it. Maybe there's no escape, whatever it is.'

The only sound is the tape as it continues to roll but he does not hear it. He is not there.

He looks at his hands, turning the palms upwards. He raises his eyes over the wheel. He cannot make sense of what he sees, the sound is muted, distant. The boy is lying in the road. That's too far away, he thinks.

He sees the bloody smear on the glass, still hears bone and

windshield crack again as the silence breaks. Shouts from the street, fists on the van, footsteps, people rushing to the dead boy. Yes, he must be dead.

Someone tries to open the van door, they are angry, shouting. He is suddenly afraid. He could drive, the engine is still running, but his body won't respond. He wants to run but he knows getting out of the van is impossible. The man who was banging on the door is walking away now, towards the boy who lies in the middle of the road. The traffic is already backing up. He can hear sirens in the distance, getting louder.

He looks up at the sky. A few clouds drift overhead, the sun is still shining. It's like nothing happened, he thinks. He looks at the boy.

The boy stands in the road trying to see over the people crowded around his body. To his right the flashing lights as the emergency vehicles pull up, to his left the van, its driver looking blankly out of the cracked windscreen.

The boy remembers leaving the flat, the sun on his face on the concrete walkway, the chill of the stairwell, wiping his nose on the back of his hand and breathing in the scent of his dog, a smell that makes him think of the warmth of the animal, its ears, its nose and its eyes. He comes to the junction and walks straight across the road. He looks to his left and sees a van approaching. He does not break stride and as he steps into the other lane he realises the van will not stop. In the moment of his death he feels like a child again. He is surprised by how little it hurts, by the feeling of weightlessness, by the air passing around his limbs and body, like a bird or something, he thinks. He waits for the ground but keeps going until he is standing in the middle of the road, trying to see his body.

The people around it stop what they're doing and look around, some stand up. They seem confused by the sound of the dogs. Of course, the boy thinks, the dogs.

The dog jumps onto the bed after he hears the front door close, savouring the scent and warmth of the boy but finds, however hard he tries, he cannot settle. He jumps to the floor and pads into the living room where the boy's friends are either waking or trying to go back to sleep. He sniffs each one to see if he can find the source of his disquiet. It's not on any of them. It is on him. He sits and sniffs himself, No, not me, my boy. He runs to the door and begins to scramble against it, his paws slipping, he runs back to the living room, jumps first on one, then another of the boys. They sit up complaining, confused and sleepy. Then the dog hears it, feels the rip in the air, the absence, and begins to howl.

The boys all stop talking. The dog takes a breath and they can hear in the distance the sound of other dogs, many voices raised in mourning.

'What's wrong with him?'

'Is there anything out there?'

'No,' says the one from the window. 'I can't see anyth...'

The dog turns one way then another, begins chasing around in circles, barking, becoming frenzied. They think he's playing at first.

'He's going mental.'

'What's up, boy, what's up?' asks the boy in the armchair, leaning forward. The dog turns and leaps, the boy jumps back in the chair, finds himself pinned by paws in the hollows beneath his shoulders, back paws on his thighs, the breath of the dog, its saliva, in his face and the dog barks, barks, is barking and the boy can feel the fear, the warning, Danger. Danger. Hurt. Run.

'What is it?' he asks quietly. 'What is it? Good boy.'

Danger. Danger. Hurt. Run. Good boy. Good boy. I am a good boy, I am a good boy, I am a good boy. Then abruptly the dog stops, remains where he is, panting doggy breath in the boy's face. The boy strokes his head, tenderly.

'What was all that about? Get down now, good boy.'

The dog leaves the boy, returns to the floor, head on front paws, eyes moving from face to face, tail thumping once, twice on the floor more in search of reassurance than enthusiasm.

A phone rings. The boys, the dog, all jump, only realise the silence once it is broken.

'Answer,' he says to himself. 'Just answer the fucking phone.' He ends the call. He knows he has to be there soon but even now he doesn't know if she's still waiting. His life is about to fall apart and he's just sitting here in this fucking car in this fucking traffic jam while they fuck about with that pointless fucker who's obviously fucking dead. At least the fucking dogs have shut up.

He undoes his seat belt and leans out of the window.

'For fuck's sake, hurry up,' he shouts.

Heads turn. A man breaks away from the small group around the boy and walks towards the car.

'What's your problem, man?'

'Look, I know this is bad, but can't we get a move on? I've got to be somewhere. Now.'

The man stops by the car window. 'The boy is dead. You will have to wait. Show some respect.'

'Perhaps if he had some then he wouldn't be dead.'

'What does that mean?'

'Well, everyone knows kids like that just take the piss.'

'And for that he deserves to die?'

'He's not helped himself, has he?'

'Unbelievable, can you hear yourself?'

The driver does not listen as the man continues. He knows he is too late, that he cannot change things. He makes a brief inventory of what he has lost and then he returns to now, to the man who refuses to see his point of view.

'All I'm saying is that some people bring it on themselves.'

The man stops talking. He blinks in the sun. It is too bright, he cannot see clearly. The colours are washed out except for the blood. He can see it wherever he looks. He cannot understand what is more important than the boy. Why can't this stupid man in his car just shut up and show some courtesy for the dead.

'I mean, some people don't know how to behave, do they? That lot certainly don't.'

The driver is surprised at the strength of the man, by the size of his hands as he reaches in and grabs him by his shirt, What did I say, passing through his mind, lifting him so his head hits the window frame. He begins to struggle with the second effort to pull him from the car but the man is too strong, holds him too tight, dragging him out by his belt, his shirt, pulling it over his head so he cannot see the first punch coming, knocking him against the car. As he tries to lower his arms more blows come. He can taste the blood, hear the cries around him and then he is on the ground. He is unaware of others joining them; some to pull the man away, others act as a shield. Some try to attack the man, others try to defend him. Those who see the phone footage later will be breathless at the speed with which the scene disintegrates.

A car appears from a side street and drives into the crowd, then another breaks from the queue and crashes into the first. People are hurled, pinned, crushed. The numbers swell, vehicles are abandoned, bystanders are drawn in. A helicopter appears overhead as the police arrive and quickly realise the situation is already beyond them, calling for reinforcements as they withdraw. They are powerless for now as they watch ordinary people smash into one another. In the midst of it all a small group try to protect the paramedics who are trying to protect the body of the dead boy, who stares in disbelief at what he has left behind.

The sirens grow louder.

The phone stops ringing. The boys, the dog, are still.

From the window one says, 'Helicopter. Want to see what all the fuss is about?

Lewis is dreaming.

In his dream he awakes to find his bed surrounded, his bedroom filled with people, shoulder to shoulder, front to back, pressed against each other, all wearing the same clothes, the same face. He shouts, terrified, What do you want, but they remain silent. He knows without leaving his bed that the flat is full, every space taken, kitchen, bathroom, living room, hallway, stretching out along the balcony, every balcony, above, below, opposite, and down the stairwells in either direction, filling pavements, streets and parks as far as the eye can see. He knows they are full, with every face turned toward him, as if he is an object of worship, except they have not come here to praise him. All he thinks is, I am a good boy, I am a good boy and he is alone in a windowless room, a clock ticking louder and louder in his chest. A voice says, I told you so, and as the explosion lifts him up into light, he wakes to a deafening bloom as a firework ricochets off the building, eyes wide, heart racing, sparks cascading past his window and he wonders if he's still dreaming, then the room returns to darkness and he remembers.

He remembers reaching the street and then running, running, the rest of the day running, through streets, through shops, down alleyways, driven by fear turning to rage as they plunged headlong into a crowd they could not avoid, desperate to keep moving lashing out at anyone who was in their way, and the noise, the constant noise of alarms and rage.

The sound of the chaos below reaches him through the open window as his hearing returns. He leans forward and looks down. Breaking glass and flaming petrol, flares and fireworks shot through the mist at the police lines. The screams and cheers, the chants and shouts, the innocent pop and clink of tear gas canisters as they are fired and discarded. The city has become a sinister carnival.

Running across a road with his friends in front and behind, feeling the car clip the sole of his trainer, sending him spinning to the ground and then his friends behind him not being there anymore, his friends in front disappearing with the panicked crowds as they fled. Standing and seeing the bodies, trying to understand, to make sense of it. A moment of stillness. Then tires squealing as the car reversed back towards him and he ran again and didn't stop running until twilight and he closed the door behind him and fell exhausted onto the bed and, despite himself, fell into a deep sleep. He ran for hours it seemed, the dog at his heels, the only one left, all his friends gone. The dog.

'Shit.' Where is he?

He gets off the bed and walks into the living room. A flare illuminates the room. The dog is there, sleeping at the feet of his dead friend.

'Glad you could make it,' says the dead boy.

Lewis is unable to move or speak.

'It's alright, I'm still getting used to it too. Sit down. Please.'

Lewis sits in the nearest armchair, his legs giving way at the last.

'Want to know what the funny thing about it is? I was going to leave. I'm booked on the train for this morning. Got my bag packed and ready in the other bedroom so I wouldn't even have to go home.'

'Why?'

'Why? Are you fucking mental? You've been outside, I've seen you. A hit and run and the place falls apart. It's just shit, lies. This isn't for me. This is just an excuse to fuck things up so someone far lazier than you or me can say, "Look at that lot, they don't deserve nothing." No respect for the living, none for the dead. Why save yourself when it's so easy to fuck it all up and say, "I couldn't help it." Sorry, Lewis. It's not easy being dead, watching people just fuck things up because they don't know any other way. I mean, why are they burning shops where they live? It don't make no sense. You alright? Say something.'

'What's it like? I mean, sorry, it's, but, what?'

'I don't know either, I'm not even sure I'm supposed to

be here. I've not seen anyone else like me about. It's funny really, because you know, you absolutely know that none of this matters afterwards. None of it. The pain, the suffering, the love, none of it matters, none of it's important. It's all the same, it just is.'

'Shit.'

'I know. Don't tell anyone for fuck's sake. You think of the mad shit people get up to when they think there are consequences, imagine what it'd be like if they knew there weren't any.'

'It'd upset your Mum.'

'All that praying for nothing. She'd go spare. Don't forget though, even though none of it matters, it's all important, how you live and that. It's important to try, you know, to try and be good.' They fall quiet. 'That was a bit awkward.'

'What, the quiet bit or talking to a dead man?' They both smile.

'What's that behind you?'

Lewis turns to look over his shoulder and by the time he looks back his friend is gone. He sits for a moment then rises, goes over and touches the chair, waves his hand in the air where his friend was sitting. The dog looks up at him. Lewis shakes his head and runs his hands over the dog's ears. 'Are you going to start talking now?' The dog just looks at him.

'Good. Good boy. None of that spooky shit.'

Lewis straightens and tries to work out what's troubling him. It's the light. How can it be morning already? He returns to the bedroom and looks out of the window. The street below is quiet, debris from the night before everywhere, but quiet. He goes back to the living room, stares at the chair where his dead friend sat, the faint scent of something metallic in the air.

'I've got to get out,' he says to himself as he pulls on a jacket and puts his hood up. 'Stay there,' he says to the dog as he opens the door. The dog is too tired to follow and watches as he closes the door.

The smell of smoke and petrol is everywhere, broken glass and bricks cover the deserted street. As he rounds the corner he catches the tail end of a police van as it passes by. He ducks back and moves again when he's certain it has gone. He's not going anywhere, just walking for the sake of it, hoping there'll be some sense to it all by the time he gets home though knowing there probably won't be.

It just is.

He crosses the road, smiling as he uses the zebra crossing, and as he does so he hears a car slowing. He looks up as it comes to a standstill. He can hear to motor ticking over. He cannot see through the darkened windshield but the dents in the bodywork tell him it is not waiting out of courtesy.

He steps off the crossing into the middle of the road.

He steps off the crossing into the middle of the road and thinks, Enough.

He steps off the crossing into the middle of the road and waits.

TO SUDDEN SILENCE WON

JACQUELINE GITTINS

In 1930s rural Ireland, ten-years-old Nèall, lives an uncertain life in abject poverty under the brutish dominance of his father. He sees himself, the oldest son by some years, as the protector of his beloved mother and siblings against his father's rage and the disdainful condemnation of his immediate community.

His drunken father causes a terrible fire. Nèall survives but is badly burnt and loses everybody he loves. Everything good in him is burned away. He leaves his father and faces the world alone, grief-stricken and embittered, on a road to his own destruction, devastating everyone he meets in his wake.

Calcine

That night, he lifted me through the open window of a house and told me to find money. It was a good house; there were lampshades, rugs on the floor, ornaments. Things placed just for the pleasure of them.

As he had told me to, I rattled any tins and pots on the dresser. Sure enough, one held coins and notes. I took the tin and had a quick look round for what he called 'grab and get outs.'

But the house was so fine, everything she would want, that I lingered and tried a door. The larder! And such a larder! Full. I stuffed sugar and tea for her in my pockets. There was fat cut from a newly butchered pig with some meat on it still.

'Boy! Make haste!'

I tucked the fat into my trousers and beneath my shirt. I found two bottles of whiskey and ran for the window, handing them out to him.

'Ah, good, good,' he said, cradling them.

'Money?'

I passed the tin out. He shook out the cash and threw the tin over the opposite hedge. He was almost gone before I climbed back out, leaving me alone in the darkening lane. Thankfully, he'd not noticed that I had wasted time, risked getting him caught, to steal unsellable food.

Ma looked over us as we lay on the mattress that bled straw through her raggedy stitched seams. She saw I was still awake and smiled.

'Look at you all, calves in the hay barn you are.'

Her eye was darkening, half closed. He had slapped her because his tea was cold. But then, I'd said, 'It wasn't cold when she gave it to you. It wasn't for you anyway.'

She got between us, took the punch, and more.

Her movements were stiff as she bent to wipe Alby and Clodagh's wet faces with the sleeve of the coat over us. Finn's breath still came in shuddered gulps, even as he slept, his head on damp-darkened rags. I took his arm from my neck and sat up. She got in with us, and we huddled for the soft touch of each other. My arms about her didn't stop her trembling.

They never did.

'Kevin Barry, fuck the English, bastards all… for the cause of Liberty,' slurred and pitched from the yard. He came into the house, singing-crying, stumbling and swearing. I heard our tin plates hit the stone floor and looked anxiously at Ma and the wee ones. They had not awoken.

'Where are you now, bitch?'

The candle he held lurched his shadow up the ladder to our attic room.

'You're up there then. Bitch with her whelps…'

I heard his boot hit the bottom rung and got ready to push the ladder and him away.

'…God, I need a piss.' He stumbled outside.

I climbed down quickly.

The food I'd got us was on the fire. Fat and sugar flames

roared out of sight up the chimney. I locked the door against him, barring it with a chair to be sure to keep him out.

I sat at the foot of the ladder, on guard. He would not warm himself on our hunger, nor would he hurt them again tonight.

But, I slept.

Through the crackle of burning thatch.

Through the poison seeping through broken bricks.

Through them going from sleep to Tech Duinn.

I woke, choking on thick gagging smoke. I couldn't see, couldn't breathe. Something fell across my back, my shirt flamed. I rolled to put it out. The door caved in. I heard the chair scraping back.

'There's one of them here,' someone shouted.

I was in a man's arms, being carried out into the air.

'Careful, careful, he's hurt, put him on his stomach, gently now.'

'In the attic,' I screamed. 'They're in the attic.'

Through the smoke, the red and black talons of smouldering roof beams clawed at the moon. They looked up at them, and then one to the other.

He was in the outhouse, stupefied. His trousers down, covered in piss.

Miss Lynch was the one that saw to the dead in our village. Mrs Coyne had lent an empty cottage for the laying out and Wake, and for me and him to stay in, while I healed.

I lay on a couch in the parlour. Ma was on the table, under a pure white linen sheet. Finn and the little ones lay on a single armchair dressed in flowered cloths. I hoped Clodagh's was the pink one.

Seeing me awake, Miss Lynch nudged her head at Mrs Coyne, who came over and put her hand on my head.

'You rest now, A leanbh.'

'My child,' she said. As Ma always did.

She pulled the scullery curtain closed, but not quite.

I was laid on my front. By shifting slightly, I could see through the gap in the curtain. Miss Lynch stood before the armchair, she lifted the pretty cloths partly off and shuddered. Mrs Coyne leaned into her; their hands went to their mouths, their arms about each other.

'Holy Mothe…' Miss Lynch nudged her hard.

They crossed themselves.

Miss Lynch knelt before the armchair with her bowl and washcloths. A pile of sweet-smelling linen was at her side. She cut some of it into strips and laid them, one by one over the arm of the chair. Three times she kissed her fingers and lowered them, bowing her head. She moved like she was arranging bouquets of flowers. So carefully wrapping each of them in the fresh white linen.

The candles lit her eyes as the full moon does on a rippled pond. When she was done, she sank back onto her heels and crossed herself.

They lay like spools of flax awaiting the loom.

The length of her did not reach either end of the table. Her breadth took no more than two of its narrow planks. They washed and dressed her in somebody else's clothes. There was lace. I saw her hair breaking as they brushed it, but still, they arranged it. Mrs Coyne took a little slide from her own hair and gave it to her.

'There, she's beautiful,' they said and laid a fresh cloth across her face. They placed a shawl about her shoulders. I was glad of that. The room was cold. The women placed sprigs of lavender at her hands. They lay the babies in each of her arms and Finn on her belly, his head against her breasts, his legs drawn up as a newborn's, like the unborn that lay beneath him.

They were ready, as revered in death as they were reviled in life. It was Mrs Coyne that slapped Finn for stealing a handful of apples from the thousands in her orchard. Herself, that told Mrs. Murphy not to trust Ma. That she would steal when she cleaned; and she never did, never.

They went around the cottage, drawing all the curtains and covering mirrors, closing all the doors. They lit candles before a picture of the Holy Mother, with her loving face, her arms outstretched as if to gather in. They pulled back the scullery curtain and held their vigil, drinking tea.

Mrs Coyne watched awhile and then nodded over at me

'He's a big boy for what, ten?' She said it kindly.

'He's built strong, like his Ma's brothers,' Miss Lynch said and smiled at me.

'Aye, I remember them,' Mrs Coyne said. 'She'd not be on

that table but for Passchendaele.'

'She would not, nor the báibíns. And him,' she nodded towards me, 'not born to her at thirteen.'

'The poor boy looks quare sore,' Miss Lynch said. She went and picked up the sheet that had covered my Ma, cut off a corner and brought it over. 'Put this on his back. The cloth that has been wrapped around a corpse is a cure.'

Mrs Coyne tried to lay the cloth with Ma's death on it, on me. Bile filled my mouth. I spat it at her. She screamed and ran to the jug and bowl, dabbed angrily at her clothes, then paused, pointing from me to them.

'In front of your poor dead Ma and the báibíns too. You're still the animal, so you are.'

I was about to say sorry, but then she said.

'The same as his Da.'

The bile I swallowed quelled the fury in my stomach to a quiet rage. She would pay for that.

'Where's himself?' Miss Lynch asked.

Mrs Coyne shrugged and shook her head.

I knew where he was. He was downing sympathy whiskeys in the pub.

The women slept in their chairs.

The shrouded shadow that was all of my kin lengthened on the wall. One by one, the candles guttered, and the darkness took them. I couldn't get up and go to them.

Face down; I shed my last boy's tears.

He was all that was left, and I hated him. Mrs Coyne's cottage was defiled by him and his filth. The good-hearted people of the village had kept him drunk for two weeks. There would be no headstone for their single grave.

To the sound of his jagged-breath sleep, I left.

The gravestone shadows point as sundials for the passing hours. The black church spire points to the scudding clouds and crescent moon that sails the shifting tide of night; netting fields and hedgerows in its wake.

She will come.

They said the last to be buried guards the graveyard until the next one comes.

I will wait. One last night, I will wait.

The thin new skin on my back parted as he dragged me from the bushes where I crouched. I cried out.

'Stop your snivelling, you soft little bastard,' he said.

His ready punch faltered as I squared up to him, but he grabbed my lapels, pulling me closer to his snarl.

'Why do you sleep in the fucking graveyard?'

'To see Ma!' I spat it in his face.

He dragged me to the mound of them and climbed on it as if he walked the earth a giant.

'Burned. Dead. Gone.'

He stamped at every word, his boot crushing the daisies I'd put there.

'She's not coming back to you; she wouldn't want to.' He drew a deep, malevolent breath. 'She's burning. Again. Burning in the flames of hell, as all whores will do.'

His face, his words, his hate. I felt the puke rising and ran, retching, to the hedge. His laughter followed. It was as my eyes lit upon a fallen branch that he shouted:

'Run, go on, run, you cripple back whore's bastard.'

He threw his dog end on the grave and walked away, still laughing. I caught him up and crashed the branch into the back of his head. And then up and down his back as he ducked and swore. He was wasted thin, weak from the drink and eaten away by spite. He couldn't grab the branch or stem my fury and backed away.

I knelt to smooth out the badge of his boot off them, and he crept back to beat me. As his shadow fell across them, I stood, swiped him in the face and lifted the branch high. A chill crept over me, and I lowered my arms, dropping the branch to the ground. He raised his fists again. Something in my face stopped him. He stared at me hard for a moment or two, his fists lowering.

'You mad bastard you.' He said it quietly before walking quickly away, looking back at me over his shoulder.

That last time we set eyes on each other, it was his that were afraid. I fell to the ground, only then feeling the wounds on my back. And, that they were weeping.

THE LANTERN MAN

VICTORIA HATTERSLEY

The Lantern Man is a novel set in the Cambridgeshire Fens, concerning the disappearance of a teenager, Alfie – an unusual, talented boy who suffered from achromatopsia, a rare form of colour-blindness. The main action takes place in 2010 when Tommy, the protagonist – now 30 – returns to the village in which he grew up after a long absence and tries to find out what happened to his best friend 15 years ago. Alfie's brittle, distant sister Diana also becomes involved in the search, although the relationship between the two is strained.

In this chapter, Tommy and Diana visit the house of a local dealer named 'Mad Pat', as they've been told by a man called Steve – whom Tommy knew a little when he was younger – that Alfie was seen in the house shortly before he went missing.

The room was stale, like the windows hadn't been opened for months. And there was this smell – a mixture of unwashed feet, takeaways and something else – something chemical that would taste bitter if you could swallow it. The air itself felt dirty, thick with flying dust particles that danced in the narrow shafts of sunlight coming through the gaps in the curtains. Tommy felt if he stayed in there long enough he would be covered in a layer of grime that would take twenty showers to remove. Mad Pat was sitting in a sunken armchair by the window, rolling a joint.

From where they were standing Tommy could see into the kitchen: chipped surfaces covered with empty cans, takeaway boxes containing fag-ends, tin foil and other assorted matter. There was an open door leading off the sitting room to the toilet and one more door, closed, which he guessed must be the bedroom. That was it: four rooms.

There were two people lying on the dubious sofa bed that covered most of the living room floor. One of them was a man with spiky red hair in a striped Freddie Kreugar-looking T-shirt who was probably in his mid-thirties but hard to tell for sure. He'd stood up, fingers twitching, when the three of them entered the room but when Pat shook his head he'd sat down again and pulled the stained duvet over his legs. The other person was a young girl with black hair and a fringe who couldn't have been more than 15. Looked like a nice enough kid – out of place here, though, like she'd walked into the wrong picture. There was an old episode of Columbo on the TV and the two of them were watching it, mouths open. Joy Division was playing in the background.

Tommy, Diana and Steve had not been asked to sit down, so they stood with their backs to the wall and waited.

Finally, Pat said, 'You frightened the life out of Mark here when you came in,' he pointed to the red-haired guy on the sofa bed. 'Been a bit edgy, you see. The other day Billy Shepherd came over to have a word with me and he bolted straight out the back with a cricket bat. Jumped over the fence. I didn't see him until two days later. Got the Fear, didn't you Mark?'

The red-haired man scowled. Pat gave a dry, crackling laugh that turned into a cough and then he licked the paper on his joint: 'Want something from me I take it then, Steve? And who are your two new friends?'

Next to Tommy and Diana, Steve shifted his feet and sniffed loudly.

'Not right now – need to wait till Tuesday, don't I? It's like I said, these two here just wanted to ask you something Pat. They're OK. You might remember Tommy here from a long time ago actually. Used to come into the Bull for a while.'

'I usually make it my business to remember people if I need to. Can't say young Thomas here rings a bell though.'

He kept his eyes down as he said this, twisting the end of the joint. 'I don't want to be terribly rude but you might want to tell me why you're here. I have a lot of guests in and out.' He stuck it between his dry, cracked lips and sparked it up.

'It's alright, we weren't going to stay long,' said Tommy, his voice sounding unusually low to his ears.

He thought about another of the stories someone had told him about Pat once, in the pub. There was that guy who'd been put in a car and driven out to some fields beyond the town and set fire to and everyone knew Pat had made it happen except nobody could prove it. Besides, the guy had been a dickhead anyway, or so everyone said. The last time Tommy had seen Pat he'd been thinner but now the bottom half of his face was all jowls, surrounded by sparse, sandy hair like Tom Petty.

'So,' muttered Pat, blowing smoke into the air, 'I'm not used to people such as yourself dropping in.' He managed a kind of theatrical bow from his chair. 'To what do I owe the pleasure, young Thomas?'

'It's about a friend of mine.'

'Is that so? What kind of a friend? There are all sorts in my experience.'

Tommy swallowed. 'It was an old friend. I haven't seen him for a long time, not since he was a teenager. He was the same age as me. It's just I'd heard from Steve that he might have been here once, years and years ago. You'd know him if you saw him. He was – well, he stood out I suppose.'

'Do I look to you like the kind of person who makes a habit of hanging around with teenagers? I feel I ought to be offended.'

'No.'

'You know you shouldn't rely too much on what Steve here

says, don't you? He's full of nonsense. Here. Have some of this.'

He passed the joint to Tommy. There was blood on the end. He put it into his mouth and took a hasty drag, before offering it to Diana who stared at it, then him.

'Alright,' he muttered, passing it to Steve, who took it and sucked it down like an asthmatic fighting for breath sucks on their inhaler.

At this point there was an urgent knocking at the door. 'Pat,' said a voice from the other side. 'Pat, for fuck's sake let me in.'

'Get that would you?' said Mad Pat to red-haired Mark on the sofa, who sprang up and began to unfasten the various locks and chains on the door. The second it was opened a skinny man burst through the door, followed by a skinnier woman. He didn't wait to say hello before pushing past Tommy and running into the bathroom.

'I've shat myself,' he said. 'There's more on the way. We've got the money now, Pat.'

This was followed by moaning noises and the sound of someone's insides exploding. The bathroom door hadn't been closed properly and now an evil smell wafted out towards them. The skinny woman with hollow eyes who had followed him in put her arms around Pat's neck in an ingratiating sort of way.

'You knew we'd get it for you didn't you darling? Can we use the back room?'

'If you like,' he said. 'It's in the usual place with your name on it.'

She gave him a kiss on the cheek and went through the door at the back, which Tommy had guessed led to the bedroom.

'I don't know where my manners are these days,' said Pat. 'Does anyone want tea? Mark, make tea. The pot's clean. And bring the Hobnobs.'

Mark rolled his eyes very slightly but got up again to do what he was told.

'Actually Pat,' said Tommy, trying to talk and hold his breath at the same time. 'You don't need to bother about tea. If you just look at this picture then...'

'Don't be a dafty, who doesn't like tea?'

The tormented groans from the toilet had stopped now. Then there was the noise of someone trying but failing to flush the chain. After a couple of attempts the skinny man came out naked from the waist down. Tommy looked away quickly but when he glanced at Diana he saw she was staring expressionlessly at his flaccid cock and pale legs covered in bruises and track marks.

'Toilet's broken Pat,' he said. 'I had to throw my pants out the window.'

'Oh for goodness' sake,' said Pat. 'I only had it fixed the other week. She's in there,' he added, nodding towards the bedroom. And then added, 'And remember what I said this time, won't you?'

The man nodded: 'Sure thing, Pat,' and went to join the other one.

There was silence for a time, broken only by the sound

of the kettle boiling and the clattering of cups and saucers. Then the red-haired man reappeared with a silver tray laden with an enormous willow-patterned teapot and several cups of differing sizes.

'Ah, marvellous. Shall I be mother?' said Pat.

'For God's sake...' said Diana. Tommy looked at her.

'What is it, my dear?'

'We don't need tea.'

'Do you enjoy football, Thomas?' said Pat, pouring tea from the pot with a practiced flourish.

'I wouldn't say I was a huge fan.'

'I used to play a bit myself, in my younger days. Goalkeeper was my position, like Albert Camus. It's a very existential position, goalkeeper.'

'I suppose so.'

'Isolated, you see. We're all isolated, aren't we, when it comes down to it? None of us can really rely on anyone else, you know. Especially not those of us who don't really fit into society, whatever that means. What is it though, society? That's what I ask you.'

He's enjoying himself, thought Tommy. There was a shout from the next room, followed by a thud and a scream, and then a low wail.

'Do you know,' continued Pat, 'the more I listened to David Icke, the more I used to think the man was right about those lizards.'

'The queen's one of them.'

'Shut up Mark.'

Tommy heard the woman shout: 'What was that for?'

'In my muscle,' the skinny man shouted out. 'You've injected the whole lot into my muscle you bitch. What am I going to do now? Alright for you now you've sorted yourself out isn't it?' There was the sound of something being thrown, or someone falling.

'Excuse me a moment, boys and girls.'

Pat heaved himself up from the armchair with a sigh and went into the next room, hitching up his tracksuit bottoms which had fallen down a little too far to expose a hairy crevice, gleaming with sweat. From the next room, Tommy could hear him talking in a low tone and accompanied by the sound of whimpering. Then he heard the woman's voice, slightly raised.

'He was only a little boy and they took him away from me.'

There were more murmuring sounds, and then silence for a moment before Pat reappeared in the sitting room.

'I do apologise, all sorted now,' he said.

The bedroom door was ajar now and Tommy could see the woman was holding a hand to her mouth, which was pissing blood. He winced. Mouths bled so much, didn't they? The man was filling a needle with something. Then the woman saw Tommy observing her.

'What the fuck are you looking at?' She kicked the door closed.

Pat tutted. 'So then, Thomas, do you take milk? What about this young lady?'

'Yes. Pat, would you mind looking at a picture for me? Honestly, I don't want to keep you long. I just want to see if you recognise my friend.'

In desperation, he thrust the picture under Pat's nose.

'It's this guy. He had black hair and he always wore sunglasses. Always. He had to.'

Pat smiled. 'Handsome lad. Well that's hard to tell. What do you say, Mark? Do you recognise this young man?'

Mark shuffled over and looked at the picture; for a moment Tommy thought he saw something flicker in his eyes, but then he shrugged, shook his head and sat back down again.

'Where are you from anyway, young Thomas?' said Pat.

Tommy told him the name of the village.

'Now where have I heard of that recently?' Pat paused, like he was thinking but in an exaggerated sort of way – if a person could think in an exaggerated way. 'Ah yes, they found a body there a few months ago didn't they? Are you sure that wasn't your friend?'

His tone was slightly mocking. Although they weren't touching, Tommy felt Diana physically tense next to him and he went to put his hand out. He felt her move. Then the young girl on the sofa bed got up suddenly.

'I'm going to be sick,' she said. She bolted into the ravaged bathroom, followed by Mark. Tommy saw Diana was watching after them with a strange expression on her face, like she was angry, or sad, or disdainful – or maybe a bit of all three.

'Now, sorry about all that. Oh no – I forgot to ask: does

anyone take sugar?' said Pat.

Tommy could hear retching noises.

Now the skinny man and woman emerged from the bedroom, seemingly calmer. She had wiped away the blood from around her mouth but was holding her hand to it in a dazed way, as though she couldn't quite work out why she was doing it. They dropped onto the sofa bed and lay there, gazing at Peter Falk.

'Tiff over with now is it?' said Pat. 'Young love,' he sighed and shook his head. 'It's a good thing I'm just an old romantic deep down.'

The girl and Mark came out of the toilet.

'Jesus kid, you look pale,' said the skinny man. The girl looked at the floor.

'Don't take the piss,' said Mark. 'She's feeling a bit paranoid. Come on,' he said, putting an arm around the girl's shoulder, 'let's get you out of here.'

He rummaged about under the duvet and found a pair of shoes and a parka.

'I'll be back later Pat,' he said, as he started to open the door.

'You'll have to clean that lavatory later you know?' said Pat, to Mark's departing back. Tommy saw Diana looking after them again with that same expression on her face.

'Pat,' said Tommy. 'About that picture.'

Pat turned to look at him and glanced down at Alfie's picture that Tommy was once again holding in front of him. He shook his head.

'Now listen,' he said. 'It's been nice having you here but like I said I've got some business to take care of. I'm afraid I've never seen that boy in my life.' He gave a lazy smile. 'Or if I have, it's slipped my memory.'

'That's my brother,' snapped Diana. She'd been quiet up to this point but clearly she'd now lost her patience. 'Can't you see this – person is playing with us Tommy? We're wasting our time.'

There was a silence as all the eyes in the room fixed themselves on her. Steve looked at her accusingly, as though she had let him down in some way. Tommy held his breath.

'That's all very well sweetheart,' said Pat. 'But let me tell you something, if I were you I wouldn't go chattering away about me or my business when you leave here. I'm sure you won't. Always best that way, isn't it?'

'Of course they won't Pat,' said Steve.

'No, I know they won't. Young Thomas here,' Pat nodded at Tommy, 'He's not a daft cunt. And I'm assuming his young lady isn't either.'

He stood up straight now. Tommy looked him in the eyes for the first time since they'd got there, and like he had that time many years ago he saw there was no life behind them.

'Oh for Christ's sake, I've got no reason to tell anyone anything about you,' said Diana. 'Who do you suppose would care?'

She met Pat's eyes. Diana wasn't afraid of anything. He stared back at her and then moved closer to inspect her. He put his hand under her chin and tilted it up roughly.

'Well then, and what's been happening to you?'

'What do you mean?'

Pat held her gaze for a moment and then gave another of his mirthless chuckles. 'People don't always see, do they? I understand. Well then, so we're agreed. You can go away and forget all about me and things will be better for all of us. Alright then Steve, it's been diverting but take them away with you now and don't be bringing me any more visitors unless they're actually worth my while. I'm a busy man.'

'Sure Pat, I'm really sorry.' Steve turned to them. 'Come on then.'

He was obviously keen to leave now. The two of them followed, Tommy feeling dissatisfied: Pat had recognised Alfie, he was sure of it. He didn't forget faces, he'd said it himself. As for Diana, she had a faceful of something that might have been simply murderous rage or might have been something worse than that. Hard to tell with her.

ZOLDANA: A WOMAN AND A VALLEY

ZOË FAIRTLOUGH

Tired of being mistreated by her father, young Iolanda dreams of leaving home and marrying an ice cream maker. It is 1913 in Zoldo in Northern Italy, where many are making their fortunes in the gelato business. Although war upends all her plans, it also reveals she is capable of much more. Against the backdrop of the massive Italian emigration that led to gelato's global reputation and presence, Iolanda's coming-of-age story mirrors the challenges of female emancipation and societal revolutions across Europe due to the Great War.

1913

1

Unaware of me, the boy at Nona's table chatters on, his words like crickets. '—and the road from Zoldo to Cibiana, it's opening soon, there's camions arriving stuffed with soldiers to finish it, their guns tall as trees.'

Years later, I'll remember this moment, me in my clogs outside my great-grandmother's house, snow dusting the ground, woodsmoke in the air, because nothing will ever be the same.

He helps himself to a hunk of the cake I made Nona. The door's ajar enough for me to recognise Gino from up the way, hair all sticking out, filthy legs never still enough for his poor mother to wash him, he's still nattering: '—Barba Toio says that the new road will get us to the Cadore in an hour, to new jobs, to sell our timber and nails not only to Italy but to Austria—Hungary also, says we'll be able to buy cloth and corn without having to go all the way around the mountain.'

Nona smacks at her apron. 'They've been talking about that road for years. So long as they leave me alone, they can do what they like.'

'Don't worry, Anzola, the soldiers won't find our store—Arsìera's a decent distance away,' Gino goes on between mouthfuls. 'The new road signs don't even mention the place. There's new signs throughout Zoldo, you know, at the entrances to all the villages, above and below, I thought ours were spelt wrong because they say Fornesighe, but Barba Toio says that's the Italian name, what we should say, not Asafornegise like you call it, because we're Italians.'

Nona scowls. 'Barba Toio should tase. I'm a Zoldana and I'll call my village what I like.'

That's enough standing outside. I push the door open. 'Sani, Nona.'

Gino twists round in his chair. 'Sani, Iolanda.'

I won't return his greeting, I'm family not him. I'm bringing Nona her meals so she won't have to go out in the cold, but he's the one being served like royalty. She's never treated me so highly.

Nona gestures to him to leave. He stuffs the rest of the cake into his pockets, sticks his tongue out at me, and scampers away. Birbante.

'You're friendly with him, Nona.' That she'd favour him over her own blood, it's just wrong, but she nods enthusiastically. 'He's a good boy. He is, he is.'

Gino's a thief. You can't leave a bread to cool on the windowsill that he doesn't help himself. In truth I like him, he's life itself, but I'm jealous, curious too. I put the bowl of stewed apples and a new ricotta on the table, but before I can ask her about the store, 'I have something for you,' she says.

Nona's my great-grandmother on my mother's side, baptised Angela Vittoria but most people call her Anzola vegia—old Angela, because she's old enough to remember the Austrian attack of 1848. She doesn't say much about it but if you don't let her cut in at the fountain or, God help us, you buy the last soft white roll from the baker, 'Austriaco!' that's what she brands you. Shrivelled, black clad, a faceful of wrinkles, she clasps her twisted hands together, her thumb rubbing and rubbing her palm, her rheumy eyes fixed on something far away, she appears to have forgotten what she was to give me.

'What about a soft-boiled egg to go with the ricotta?' I say, to bring her back.

'No.'

'Gino's had all the cake, Nona, you should eat something. Have some stewed apples, no need to chew.'

'Nothing wrong with my teeth.' She crosses her arms tight to her meagre chest, but truth is all she has left is gums.

She rarely eats yet she's alive, so she must allow something sometime to pass her lips. The fact is Nona's isn't like everybody: she speaks little, listens less, and has the habit of appearing unexpectedly as far away as Cibiana, a good few kilometres up the road. Come spring that's where she'll gather wild greens while we wait for our gardens to grow. 'The gamàite are best in Cibiana,' she insists, but she isn't supposed to go gathering there since our mountain regole are clear: you can forage and pasture only in the places assigned to your kin. Still, Nona's very old and strange so the people of Cibiana don't bother her with our ancient rules.

The one rule Nona does follow is her own: she won't accept anything she hasn't paid for. She uses money at the new alimentari, but in exchange for food or a shawl from me, I get buttons and flowers, a silver thimble once. 'I can't see so good to sew no more,' she said.

Now she pulls out a bit of card from the table drawer, likely payment for the ricotta. 'Here,' she flips it to me like it's nothing. 'Ta mare—that's your mother.'

The woman in the photograph sits steady against a white background, wide-set black eyes and strong eyebrows like mine too much for our face, her chin sticks out more, that or my mouth is larger, otherwise we're the same, with the same dark braids pinned over our heads. Pearl-topped hairpins frame her crown like a studded halo so the picture must have been taken on a feast day —Zoldane use those pins only on special occasions. She sits straight and strong, her capable hands in her lap my own.

Oddio me mi, I've no memory of my mother—I never saw her picture before. In my dreams she was a younger version of Nona, scrawny, stubborn and secretive, but suddenly my mother is real and immensely beautiful.

'Grazie Nona,' is all I can muster.

She shrugs. If she has a heart, she keeps it hidden.

I slide the photograph inside my bodice. That simple gift brings me closer to Nona, like how I should feel towards her, like we can trust each other. I have to ask her, 'And what's at Arsìera that the soldiers won't find?'

She glares at me. 'None of your concern.'

That just stirs up my interest. 'Dai po, Nona, what store was Gino talking about?'

Stone-faced, she shoves the tin of corn into my hand. 'My pite need feeding.' She pushes me outside and slams the door. I'm not surprised, and I'm not offended because that's what she's like, for years I've put up with her. She can scowl all she likes, I will find out her secret, but she's given me a picture of my mother, so I won't press her today.

The chickens squawk, demanding their supper, I scatter the corn in wide arcs around me and they peck at the ground like they've never before been fed.

2

The bells of San Vito's are announcing the first Angelus. Although the chapel's in the square down a way, in the stillness of winter at dawn the bells sound like they're ringing right in the house. I genuflect and pray to the Virgin Mary to watch over me, Angelus Domini nuntiavit Mariæ—, but the front door lets in a bitter chill.

Coughing thickly, Papà puts the pail of milk on the shelf. He pulls off his old cloak and hat, stamps snow off his clogs and hangs everything on the rack to dry. He sits at the hearth and stares at me. 'Don't just stand there, worse than useless, bring me the spittoon.'

It's under the bench where he left it but his twisted mouth holds a grim satisfaction in making me fetch. The congealed remnants of previous spits glisten inside the brass pot. My stomach heaves.

Noisily he clears out his lungs and rubs his hands before the fire. 'Ostia, this winter's been cold. Where the hell is spring?'

Papà doesn't talk much. Even when he appears to be listening, I think he's mostly in his own head. Anyway, he knows well as I do that spring mightn't arrive until summer, that's the way of Zoldo. Stuck in the crown of mountains as we are, the seasons can have a hard time finding us.

I set food and barley coffee on the bench by the larìn, the rough-hewn granite block that's hearth and heart of our home. New logs on the embers send smoke curls up into the chimney hood. The flames grow, their scarlet glow picking out the beaded cross on the wall and the frost etchings in the dawn window. My bones ache for sunshine.

'Give me that.' His red-veined nose twitching at the smell of bacon, he grabs his bowl and shuffles along the bench to his corner. His stockinged feet steaming on the hearth, he eats, his hands shielding his food, his head tucked between his hunched shoulders, his closed-in look is made more so by the greying beard hiding his face. 'The canyon road up from Longarone will be clear of the snow,' he mutters. 'Now we'll get everyone back as it should be.'

I'd never breathe a word to Papà but I'm counting the days for Rico to return from Naples. 'I'll see you at the end of March, bela Iolanda,' he'd said when he left for work last autumn with all the other men. 'Maybe you will,' I'd replied. I wouldn't be like those girls who'd followed him around at harvest time, geese with no self-respect, but I'd wait for him.

Rico will be back in the spring, flush with wages from his construction job, ready to settle down. That's what he said and I never did anything to encourage him. He asked me my age and I told him sixteen though I was a few months short. 'On the young side to marry,' he said, 'but a good head on those pretty shoulders.' He wouldn't have said that if he didn't have intentions. I'll make a good wife, anyone will tell you, I'm young but can manage a house and fields, animals too. I can leave home if I marry Rico, I'd have to look after his parents—that's our way, but it wouldn't be a hardship, not compared to living with Papà.

When Rico marries me, I'll go with him down to Naples in winter when he works there with his father, I'll go with him up to Salzburg in summer when he makes ice cream at his uncle's shop, I'll go over Papà's objections—he despises ice cream makers. 'Wretched gelatieri, ill-fated to roam the earth half their lives, exiled from mountain and family, forced to work among strangers, doing a woman's work at that.' I don't know the why for my father's loathing, maybe only that ice cream has brought more prosperity to some Zoldani than he's achieved. But I won't have to leave. Rico wants to build a house in Zoldo, that's what he said. He'll marry me and I'll bear his children.

I sneak out my mother's picture from inside my bodice. I feel she approves of my wish.

'Where's my tobacco? Where is it?' Papà growls behind me. 'Always daydreaming, worthless girl.'

I tuck the picture inside my sleeve and hand him the pouch from its place on the mantel.

'And the egg money?'

I've no words. That money is mine. I look after the chickens, feed them and clean after them. The women always keep what they earn from selling eggs, that's our way. But it's more our way that a daughter doesn't question her father. I put my hand in my pocket.

My blood boils as he plucks the sparse centesimi from my fingers. He owns his house and land—he earned well in his youth, carpentering in Vienna, enough to set himself up with a workshop here building everyone's barns and roofs, making balconies and shutters—he has enough money without taking mine.

His actions and insults smarting—I am not worthless— we finish eating in silence. Finally, he gets up from the bench. 'I'm going to the sawmill and choose timbers to repair Barba Gidio's staircase. Traiber's put aside some good larch for it.'

That signals that it's time for me to get back to work. 'I'll take the barrow to the mill later for a sack of flour.' I mention this just to say something but regret it as the words leave my mouth.

'What do you want, a medal?' he grunts. 'We all do our part. It's not free to live here.'

Daer, I know that. From the moment I could reason, he's made it clear that my being born female is a debt I'll never repay, but he's never understood that for a kind word I'd work twice as hard without it weighing. Resentment floods but I say nothing, a daughter doesn't backchat her father if she doesn't want the back of his hand. My finger inside my sleeve touches my mother's picture, still there.

He unfolds himself from the bench and fishes in his pocket for his pipe. 'Beh, I'm off for the timber.'

I nod but I know he's off to the tavern to sit with his friends, drink grappa and spout judgements. With my money.

He hurries down the hill, his few words cast to the wind. 'Take care of the barrow and look in at your Nona's.' That's what he says but he doesn't care about her, he doesn't care about anyone but himself.

I go upstairs to hide my mother. Stuffed in the tin among the corn leaves in the mattress, she'll be safe with my christening earrings and Nona's silver thimble.

I finish my chores, make the beds, wash the bowls in the bucket, sweep the floor, feed the chickens. I hang the pails onto my yoke and head down to the fountain in the square, past Meda Lucia's and past Dora's, past the bakery, past the sale e tabacchi that sells salt and tobacco and newspapers, and past the alimentari that sells everything else.

I stop in the shadow of San Vito's spire. Around the main plazeta of Fornesighe, the stone houses are huddled close as if curious to witness the goings-on but there's nothing much to see: Meda Lucia briskly sweeping the snowy chapel steps, Meda Rina flinging open the dairy's shutters, Barba Toio wasting his way to the tavern. I fill the pails, go and water and feed the pig down at the field, then it's back up to the fountain for the house water. If I'm quick, I'll get to my best friend Dora's in time to walk to church together. That'll be the sum of my winter Sunday, spent in the kitchen, the pigsty, and at mass—the day of any young Zoldana.

The bells are calling for me to take my place at the back of the church with the other unmarried girls. That will change, see if it doesn't. Soon I'll sit at the front with the wives. My spirits lifting, I head home.

Uphill are the blackened wood barns where we keep our beasts in winter, scattered about are the handkerchiefs of land where we grow our food in summer, the sleeping woods and forests above us, the rimy river below, the other villages beyond, the silent mountains all around, this is my world, all I ever expect to know.

3

Spring in our valley is a time of arrivals. Cliff martins swoop between roofs, snowdrops bow their milky heads, and our men return from months of work away. Weary husbands and fathers trudging along the winding road coasting the Maè River, hungry sons and brothers climbing over the steep passes, along the river and through the mountains, for centuries these have been the ways into Zoldo from the world outside.

'Amedeo's coming home,' Dora says, her whole face glowing as we walk back from church arm in arm. He's one of our carpenters returning from the rich Austrian and German cities north of us, bringing home a decent pay for a hard season's work. From the south will come those who've earned their lire in Padua, Venice, and as far as Milan, Genoa and Naples, from construction jobs or from selling roast chestnuts, zalet pastries, and spiced honey pears, the tiny ones you can eat in a bite. On foot and by cart the men will arrive in time for the spring sowing.

'And then what?' I ask, 'do you think he'll marry you?'

'No, silly, we're too young. I'm not getting married until I'm at least twenty. He has to do his military service anyway.' She squeezes my arm. 'And you, Iolanda? Do you want Rico to marry you?'

'Yes, of course, as soon as he can. He's going to build us a house on the hill up at Cornigian. A lovely white house in the sun.'

'What does your father say?'

'I haven't asked him but I'm getting married anyway.'

Dora laughs and hugs me. 'That's what I love about you.' Then her expression turns serious. 'It's an important decision, marriage, you shouldn't rush it.'

I'm not rushing anything, but I do want my life to begin, to sit at the hearth with my husband and decide what to buy with the earnings: seed, tools, a fat piglet, a cow if we can or a scrap of land to grow beans, cabbage, God willing maize and potatoes too. I want to sit at the hearth with my husband, to behold the love in his eyes when I serve him his food, to have our children climb onto my lap and wrap their arms around my neck, to live together on our land, to tend to it and live in God's glory. I want this all so much it hurts.

SHIZUKO

LLOYD MILLS

That night I offered to drive us down to the coast. 'No.' Stated so emphatically it left little doubt there would never be anymore drives to any seaside town.

That night I resolved to write you a long email so you could read it and then delete it.

The next morning, I sat in the bath for twenty-eight pages. I gently lowered my cold stiff arms into the warming welcomeness of the water. As my knees rose through the surface and my shoulders submerged, I heard a distinct 'pop' from inside my stomach. Ripples emanated as if someone had thrown a pebble into the still surface. I sat upright, not moving for ten minutes. Each little shudder aggravated the pain. I tried to shuffle down and it burned.

I slowed my breathing. I calmed myself. I concentrated on the inward and outward, whispering my special word again and again, just as you had taught me. Eventually, eventually I was allowed to step from the bath.

That night in bed I investigated. Fingers and eyes. There was definitely a small round something settled behind my navel. A new addition to my body, resting, small and compact. A remembrance?

As the weeks passed my little growth grew below my skin. My tummy was getting rounder. Simultaneously it appeared that I was getting shorter. Though invisible to the naked eye the shrinkage and enlargement were near continuous, like the growth of your hair or fingernails.

The realisation wasn't a long time coming that these disturbing phenomena occurred when I thought of you. Your long straight shining black hair, your clean, taut skin, those clear seeing eyes, that funny little cornrow in the tuft between your thighs. Shizuko, you always exuded the calm of one who is in control.

My daytime thoughts were small growth and almost imperceptible shrinkage. Night time dreams were more obvious. I tried not to think of you (night or day), but it was difficult. As difficult as emptying the mind when meditating. All those thoughts that impinge and need to be ignored. When on a mat they can come and go and one continues on, unchanged and unchanging. But these thoughts of you, they came and went and left a mark, a sign. Pop bigger, body shrinking. The longer it went on the more difficult it became to not think of you.

I started staying indoors as much as possible. And all the time I was getting rounder. Still you appeared before me. Eventually I didn't dare go out. I waddled, nearly rolling, around the house.

My skin was stretching, tighter and tighter. Paradoxically, as I grew rounder, so I got thinner. I was paper wrapped around an inflated football. Eventually I was the size of a beachball.

And still that email needed writing. Soon my arms would not reach around my stomach.

you are such an intelligent woman. i love talking discussing with you late into the night walking on the beach or sitting in the cafe. you don't overwhelm me with your intelligence you encourage me to grow. you understand my inability to construct logical arguments in the same way you understand my lack of strategy when playing chess. maybe you enjoyed the surprise element the illogicalness confronting the philosophy graduate. and i shall always be grateful for the hours and hours whole weekends weeks spent encouraging mindfulness the meditation mat that special phrase to repeat when turbulence arises. that spine of steel the inner core and strength you always consider the effect on others you work hard to ensure happiness yet you wont be pushed around. and lets not forget that you are the most attractive woman i have ever met. you said i had reawakened the sexiness in you. i never did that. i never did that, it was always there within you. you are special. don't ever forget it.

As I was disappearing into parchment, so my round growth grew in abundance. Still I slowly expanded and shrunk at the same time. Balloon-like, I rose up the wall and as a sheet I slid under the window. I floated, weighing less than the air. Away, up on the currents that all the folk down there know nothing about. I knew where I was headed and there was nothing I could do to stop it. I knew there was nothing to fear. I was as water, flowing where I needed to go. I was not drowning, I was meandering like a river confronted by individual rocks, parting and forking three, four, five individual streams and then reforming into one more powerful surging. And yet it was ineffable, weak and limp, but always liquid.

I seemed to be gathering all your learning by osmosis. D H Lawrence, Vipassana meditation, Beaker People, chess, Basho haiku. From the clouds? From you? And all the time that music. Arvo Part. Spiegel Im Spiegel. Violin and piano gently holding me aloft as if they were transparent wings, soothing, swooping, firm and gentle. Now, five thousand nine hundred and thirty-six miles from my home I knew your house as soon as it came into view. I could feel me expanding. My skin stretched over the balloon. Immediately above your chimney stack it popped. I was as brush strokes of coloured paint slowly wafting down, turning your roof and windows and walls into a smeary psychedelic wash. Safe, I was finally whole, finally empty. Understanding how we need to separate ourselves from the physical world with its dependence on material things. The emotions will calm and we will float. Don't ever forget me.

THE UNVEILERS

Susan Allott has a degree in English Literature from the University of Leeds and a Masters in Media & Communications from Goldsmith's College, London. She is a Faber Academy alumna and was longlisted for the Mslexia novel competition 2017. Susan completed the Unthank Online Fiction Workshop with Stephen Carver in Spring 2018. She lives in London with her Australian husband and their children. Interference is her first novel.

Nicholas Brodie has studied a Graduate Diploma in Editing & Publishing at RMIT University, Australia. Previously, he has moonlighted as a film critic and has been part of the anthology 100 Stories for Queensland. He recently completed Unthank's Online Fiction Workshop with Stephen Carver.

Jax Burgoyne studied the BA American Literature with Creative Writing at UEA and then moved on to a Masters there called 'Studies in Fiction' – which involved reading experimental fiction. After this grounding, plus a few years in the book-wilderness (just watching TV) she came to Unthank School and took part in the Advanced Fiction Workshop with Ashley Stokes, completing Writer, a novella, during her second session.

Carey Denton lives in Cambridge and finally decided to start writing, rather than talk about writing, some ten years ago. She was shortlisted for The Guardian Travel Writing Competition in 2011 and her piece appeared in print that November. She is currently finishing an MA in Creative Writing at Manchester Metropolitan University and hopes to complete her third novel this year.

She has attended the USW Writing the Novel with Sarah Bower and Ashley Stokes and the USW Advanced Fiction workshop with Ashley Stokes.

John Down works for a mental health charity, he is married with three daughters and lives in Norwich. He has completed the Unthank courses Introduction to Fiction with Ashley Stokes and How to Write a Novel with Stephen Carver.

Zoë Fairtlough is English by birth, Italian by childhood, and American by adoption. After a corporate career, she's raising her children, running a consulting business, and writing. Zoldana was inspired by her Italian grandmother, a gelato pioneer. Zoë has published several short stories and Love, War and Ice cream—a collection of family legends. To help her write, she finds three things invaluable: walks in the woods, Nine Mile Writers—a writing group in Philadelphia (http://ninemilewriters.wordpress.com/) — and the Online Fictions Workshops led by Ashley Stokes and Stephen Carver. Zoë has been a student with the Unthank School of Writing since 2016. Her current project is a novel about memory and inheritance.

Jacqueline Gittins is 67 and has written, sporadically, since she was a child, usually poetry. When she was thirteen, somebody sent a poem she had written about the assassination of John F. Kennedy to Jackie Kennedy. She had it published, Jacqui's first and only published work. When, despite her obvious genius, Mrs Kennedy failed to adopt her, Jacqui forgot about writing, apart from a few vague scribblings, until forty years later when she took an Open University course in Creative Writing with Ashley Stokes as her tutor, mainly writing poetry. After a few more tumbleweed years with an idea for a novel in her head, she looked for writing groups online and found Ashley was leading the Advanced Fiction Workshop. Having got a Distinction under his tutorage with the OU, she confidently signed on. From the critiques and encouragement from Ashley and her peers during the face to face readings on the course, came actual, written chapters of the hitherto intangible novel. Jacqui still attends the Advanced Fiction Workshop with Ashley Stokes

Victoria Hattersley lives in Norwich, UK, works in publishing and has a nine-year-old daughter. She has had several stories published, including 'The Girl' in Unthology 6 (Unthank Books), 'Kangaroo' in Before Passing (Great Weather for MEDIA, New York), and 'Looking for Jim Morrison' in Words and Women: Three (Unthank Books,). She has recently completed her first novel, The Lantern Man, and is now working on her second. Victoria has attended several courses at the Unthank School of Writing. She began with the Introduction to Writing Fiction course with Ashley Stokes, before which she had not written for over a decade. She has taken part in several workshop groups and also took the school's novel course, without which she is pretty certain she would not have completed a single chapter, let alone an entire novel.

Marc Owen Jones has had stories published by Unthology, Bridge House Publishing, Labello Press, Red City Review Magazine, Fresh Ink, Momaya Press, Rattle Tales and Prole Books. He has been longlisted for the Fish Prize, shortlisted for the Fish Flash Fiction Prize and nominated for The Pushcart Prize. He has attended the Advanced Fiction Workshop with Ashley Stokes.

Sabine Meier studied English and French Literature and Linguistics in Braunschweig, Germany. After working as a language teacher for more than twenty years, she did an MA in Creative Writing at Manchester Metropolitan University. She took part in Stephen Carver's course 'How to Write a Novel' and has participated in Ashley Stokes' 'Online Fiction

Workshop' since 2015. Her first novel Young is ready for publication, its sequel Walls in progress.

Lloyd Mills is a South London boy, grown via West Yorkshire, now comfortably ensconced in North Norfolk. Former archaeologist, teacher, unemployed layabout, and presently a parish clerk. Reading and writing have always been parts of his life, to greater and lesser degrees, but he's now trying more seriously to produce more complete work. He has attended various fiction writing courses led by Ashley Stokes.

Nicola Perry started out as a story liner for a fiction packagers in London before attempting a first novel. That manuscript was never published but, for those five years, she wrote feverishly, studied her craft and attended conferences in Ireland, North America (Breadloaf) and Jamaica, where she met the most amazing writers. Later, she went on to co-author a film script (optioned by WMA), has a travel book published and works with a string of amazing writers on their works in progress. For the last few years, she has been pulled between two passion projects: The Baffling Shapes of Others (a transmedia project) and the Lost Lessons of Imaginary Men (a novella). She attended the Advanced Fiction Workshop, hosted by Ashley Stokes, in Winter 2017.

Lorraine Rogerson is from Manchester. She lives in Broadstairs in Kent. She started writing when she stopped full-time work and, inspired by her experience of Arvon's residential magic, she took Stephen Carver's 'How to Write a Novel' online course in early 2016. Since May of that year she has taken part in successive sessions of Ashley Stokes's Online Writing Workshop. She has just completed an MA in Creative Writing at the University of Kent. The Shadows of Moths is her first novel.

Jose Varghese is a bilingual writer/editor/translator from India teaching English in Jazan University, Saudi Arabia. He is the founder and chief editor of Lakeview International Journal of Literature and Arts and Strands Publishers. His first book was Silver Painted Gandhi and Other Poems' (2008). His poems and short stories have appeared in journals/anthologies like The Salt Anthology of New Writing 2013, 10 Red Anthology by Red Squirrel Press, Luminous Echoes Anthology by Into The Void, Unthology 5, Chandrabhaga, Kavya Bharati, Postcolonial Text, Retreat West and Spilling Cocoa Over Martin Amis. He was a finalist in the 2018 Beverly Prize for International Writing for his short story manuscript 'In/Sane', shortlisted in the 3rd and 10th Eyewear Fortnight Poetry Prize in 2017 and the 2016 Hourglass Short Story Contest, commended in the 2014 Gregory O'Donoghue International Poetry Prize, the winner of The River Muse 2013 Spring Poetry Contest, a runner up in the 2013 Salt Flash Fiction Prize, and a second prize winner in the Wordweavers Flash Fiction Prize 2012. He is a contributing editor/writer for Panorama: The Journal of Intelligent Travel. He has attended the Online Fiction Workshop with Ashley Stokes from 2016 and is working on his first novel.

Claudie Whitaker lives in Brighton and works for an online second-hand bookshop. She is a writer of flash fiction and has been published in anthologies. She is writing her first novel. She has completed Stephen Carver's How To Write A Novel course and is a member of Ashley Stokes' Online Fiction Workshop.

Lightning Source UK Ltd.
Milton Keynes UK
UKHW021236160519
342789UK00006B/535/P